John Warren Stewig

Carthage

Torch

TORCH

Jill Paton Walsh

FARRAR STRAUS GIROUX
New York

One

I was not afraid of marrying Dio; I didn't want to, but I was not afraid of it, not, that is, until I understood that it meant visiting the old man. We were all afraid of the old man. He had chased us off the marble fields so often, waving his big stick, shouting obscure words. And there were dark stories about him. He was now very old, and could remember too much. People were afraid of what he could remember. Just the same, the boy and girl were sent to him for instruction. He told them the unmentionable things they needed to know. Sometimes he banned the match, sending word into the village. He didn't give reasons; just the words 'not those'.

But I was afraid of him because he had struck me, drawing blood across the back of both my legs as I ran, when my goats had strayed on to the marble field, and were eating the flowers that grew in profusion in the cracks of the polished stones. Only wild flowers. They grew everywhere, and the goats were welcome anywhere else. All over the dry hills and hollows, and along the banks of the river; only not among the broken marble, on the acres where the old man lived.

I would have preferred to wait to be married until the old man was dead; but I couldn't. I was already thirteen. Dio comforted me. 'He's not that bad,' he told me. 'Not all the time, anyway. I went there once with Niko, and we were playing about. We were looking for somewhere flat to run a race. We went to that long, level part of the marble fields, where the terraces and the thrones are, and we were running when he came. He wasn't angry. He sat down on one of the thrones, and clapped when Niko won.'

I assumed this was just a story Dio made up to comfort me; it didn't seem likely. And Dio wasn't particularly truthful. He liked things to be more exciting, brighter, better, or even worse, than they really were. You couldn't rely on his truthfulness, but you could rely on his kindness; I assumed he was just talking to cheer me up.

They gave us each a sip of wine in the village square, and put a white cloak round me, and a saffron one round Dio. They crowned us with wild olive, and field poppies which withered in the heat and shrivelled on our damp brows as we made the trek along the hillside, and round the Hill of Cronos, descending on the dusty track to the marble fields. I dragged my sandals, unwilling. When we came round the shoulder of the hill and saw the marble fields, lying like the stumps of a felled stone forest on the slopes down to the snake-bed of the glistening river, I was trembling. But the old man was nowhere to be seen.

We wandered hand in hand, shedding poppy petals like gouts of blood, across the broken pavements, among the fallen blocks and drums of the stone forest. There were more poppies growing in the cracks, with anenome, and iris, and paschalis, and a thousand thousand more. A stone basin lay skewed in a line of stumpy wall; it held a little dew, rapidly vanishing in the heat, and too little to drink, though I dipped the end of my hair, bunched like a brush, and laid the coolness of the wet strands against my cheek. Then I stopped again, damped the handful of hair again, and offered it to Dio. He took my hand, and held the cool wet hair against his cheek.

'Thank you,' he said. 'You have lovely hair.'

'You don't have to say that,' I said. 'You don't have to talk to me like that. I know how things are.'

6

We looked for the old man idly at first; we were not in any hurry to find him. But when we had wandered about for an hour or so, we began to worry. 'What if he isn't here?' I asked Dio.

'He's always here,' he said, frowning.

We weren't supposed to have to look for him all over the marble fields, though. He was supposed to see the cloaks of saffron and of white, and come to us. We began to search for him carefully, going up and down the pavements and among the broken walls. Separating, we each covered a patch of ground. The sun was still high, but we knew it very well; it would suddenly slide sideways behind the hills across the river, and darkness would be barely an hour off. Back in the village square they would be lighting lanterns and roasting a sheep for us.

'But what shall we do if we can't find him?' I cried to Dio, searching a little way off among a few stunted trees. 'Whatever shall we do?'

'It's all right, Cal,' he said, 'I've found him. He's here.'

But then I heard him say, more softly, as I clambered over the stones towards him, 'Or, rather, I've found him and it's not all right.'

And it wasn't. The old man was lying in a half-fallen chamber of the ruins, with his leg dramatically broken and folded, pinned under him. And he must have been there a long time. The runnel of blood on the flagstones had dried, flowed and dried again, building a nasty thickness, with a wavy edge. Flies clustered round his eyes and mouth, and walked in his nostrils. His cheeks were sunken and his eye sockets were sunken, with an arch of bone like a bridge between the hollows. He looked more dead than anyone I had ever seen before, not counting goats, but he wasn't dead; he was breathing with a rattling sound in his throat, and a shuddering heaving of his rib cage at each gasp in and out.

7

'Water,' said Dio. 'There must be some. Find it, quick.'

I found it as soon as I could. A little gushing spring ran out between two slabs of stone in a wall of a roofless room. It intruded there; when the stones were sound they would have been dry. And it had so little strength it could not even keep the flagstone floor wet very far, but spread out, died away to dampness, and burned off in the sun in a wisp of mist. All very well, but I could lay my hands on nothing much to bring it in. At last I found a piece of broken clay jar, a curved fragment like a section of eggshell, and managed to bring a mouthful in that. When the old man had taken several sips from the broken clay, Dio said, 'We'll never get him enough in that – and he must have things, somewhere – a water-jar, a blanket. Sit with him while I look.'

'No, let me look,' I said. 'I don't want to stay here without you.'

'You aren't afraid of him like this, are you?' said Dio.

'Yes. No. I just don't want to stay. I'll look.'

'Baby!' said Dio. 'Go on then.'

And that did take time, because the old man's den was well hidden. It was a corner of a fallen house, under a roof of sticks and straw. He had a brushwood bed, and a chipped white water-jug, and a cold hearth, and a blanket made of sheep's skins roughly sewn. He had so little that it was clearly going to be easier to bring his house to him than to bring him home to it.

We ran to and fro, and Dio struggled to fix a shelter, a layer of skins lying on brushwood, propped across the broken walls above the old man's head. As we worked the sun skidded suddenly below the western horizon, and lit a dying fire in the western sky. I was already lost; the track back to the village, along the hillsides, across the screes and through the beds of little torrents was too dangerous in darkness. We would miss our own wedding feast.

*

8

At first, and I hope the mountain gods were watching it, we spared no time to think of our own disaster. The old man was dying. We made him warm, we propped his head, we lit a fire and made a brew of thyme and marjoram, and a bitter little plant my mother showed me which eases pain, and I sat beside him and lifted little scoops of the infusion to his lips in the curved shard of clay. Dio tended the fire and tried to catch something to eat, though lizards were all he managed.

In the deadest darkness, beyond the faintest aftermath of sunset, before the smallest prophetic gleam of dawn, the old man began to talk.

'You must stay here,' he said, looking at Dio. 'Somebody must stay here. You needn't bury me; there's a dry well you can drop me down, and a coverstone to put on it. But you will have to stay.'

'I can't do that,' said Dio, reasonably. 'I'm supposed to marry Cal, and plant olive trees. If they'll still let me, after this,' he added, and then frowned, looking at me, as if he wished he had not spoken that thought. He needn't have troubled himself, it had already occurred to me. A night spent alone with a boy would disgrace and unfit any girl. You were supposed to have the ceremony the evening before, not the morning after doing that. We could explain, of course. Would that help? I doubted it, somehow.

'You must stay,' the old man was saying to Dio. 'Guard the treasure. I have been Guardian since I was eighteen. I make you the Guardian after me.'

'What treasure?' said Dio. 'I never heard of any treasure here.'

'Secret from the village,' the old man said. He struggled to prop himself up, and we helped him manage it. The fever had cooled a little, and his eyes were brighter. 'Some of the older ones would remember . . . but it was famous. A famous thing. There has to be someone here in case they come for it . . .'

'They? Who? Nobody comes,' said Dio.

'Can you blame them?' I asked. 'When you think how we treat strangers . . .'

'They haven't come for a long time,' said the old man. He seemed to be tiring himself, trying to talk to us. 'Not for many years . . . not in my time . . .'

'You want me to stay here on the marble fields, in your place, waiting for somebody to come who hasn't come for, what? sixty years?' Dio sounded wondering, incredulous, and yet he spoke gently.

'Longer,' said the old man, once more trying to sit up a little, and groaning. 'Not since the manhood of the Guardian before me.'

'I couldn't be Guardian if I didn't know anything about it,' said Dio. I looked up at him, startled, and saw from a certain tenderness in his expression that he was sorry for the old man and was humouring him. I could think of a goodly number of reasons why Dio could not be Guardian on the marble fields that seemed more powerful to me than his lack of knowledge.

'Ago,' the old man began, 'in the time when we had boxes in our hands which sang and talked to us from far away, when the mechanical birds carried people over mountains and across oceans, and pictures shone many miles, and journeys were made by lighting fires inside carts instead of hitching donkeys . . .'

'Yes, yes,' said Dio, losing patience. All our stories began like this; every old crone in the village could spin a long tale about Ago. He couldn't cut short the old man. 'When men had returned from the moon, and out of grains of sand had made machines to think and write and work the abacus . . .'

'Yes!' cried Dio. 'We know about Ago. Tell about the treasure.'

'It was already ancient then,' said the old man. 'Give me

another sip of the balm, girl.' I did so. 'It was already done in memory of other times, centuries before Ago.'

'What was?' said Dio. Softly, hungrily.

'Lighting the torch,' the old man said. 'Every four years, lighting one of the torches, and carrying it away over the hills . . .'

'Where to?' I asked.

'To the Games. Wherever they were.'

'Old man, you will be dead on one of your next breaths,' said Dio, sharply, 'and we do not understand you at all. You are asking me to do something, and you must explain it, quickly, before it is too late!'

The old man understood that. He shook his head, as though to clear cobwebs from before his eyes. 'Long ago they came every four years,' he said. 'They had a name for a space of four years – the time between one Games and the next. That was called an Olympiad: called for this place, these stones. They took the torches and ran with them. It mattered very much. Now there is one torch left, and the bowl for lighting it. If ever they come again, they must be shown where these things are hidden. There has to be a Guardian. You, now.'

'Very well,' said Dio. 'Where are the things hidden?'

'You will find them . . .' he said. He closed his eyes, and sighed heavily. His head rolled on the bracken pillow.

'Wait!' I wailed at him, shaking him hard. 'Wait! We are supposed to have your word that we may marry! What will become of me? You are supposed to tell us the secrets . . .'

He opened his eyes very slowly, as though the lids were weighed down with stones. 'It's all right with you two,' he said, in a voice that had died to a whisper, 'you're not too close.'

'But what do we do?' I asked.

'You know what the goats do,' he said, very weary. 'Do that.'

Two

He spoke not a word to us after that, though he waited till sunrise to die. The great golden disc of the sun slid over the skyline, while the fields of heaven glowed primrose with a rim of poppy red round the hilltop, like the rosy edge of a human finger held up to the light. A bird sang loudly in the Judas tree. The old man sighed, and stopped the painful rackety breathing we had been listening to all night. We walked away from him and sat down apart, each looking at the rising morning across the valley, each alone.

When he spoke to me, Dio said, 'Did we do right? Could we have saved him?'

'I don't think so, Dio. We could have run back to the village, but we couldn't have brought help in time. Of course we did the right thing.'

'But if I had thought of you, Cal, we would have left him and gone back. Now I don't know . . .'

'How could we have left him? There wasn't anything wrong with me. Do you think I would have liked you to just leave him there lying on his leg? I wouldn't have left one of my goats like that.' I shuddered then, mentioning goats.

'Cal, what shall we do?' Dio asked.

'I'm supposed to do what you tell me,' I said, unkindly.

'We didn't make it. I'm not your husband yet, and I'm asking you.'

'We shall have to go back. Then you will be given another girl, and my family will deal with me.'

'What will they do?'

'How do I know? Has anything like this ever happened before?'

We fell silent, both, I imagine, remembering the scandal when Lalla ran off with George. 'We haven't done anything wrong,' he said, in a while.

'What difference will that make?' I wondered. And then we heard voices, footfalls, light and rapid, on the terraces above us on the slopes, and Niko appeared, running. Seeing us, he stopped in a shower of dislodged pebbles scuffed up under his feet, and though Dio had jumped up, alarmed, and laid a finger to his lips, Niko put his hands to his mouth and hallooed loudly, 'Youreeka! They're here!'

But Niko hadn't brought the village elders, or our parents. Only other children, full of curiosity, who had come scrambling round the hillside to find us. Five of them, Niko apart. Two big boys, nearly our age, Vryon and Peri, and two little girls, Athie and Cassie, and Athie was holding her baby brother Lukas, slung in a shawl on her back. They crowded round us, clamouring, all talking at once. We quickly understood one salient point – a party of villagers would be coming to fetch us, to 'deal with us' as soon as the animals were herded and fed, and the necessary work put in hand.

'How long have we got, Peri?' asked Dio. I noticed that it was Peri he asked, though Vryon was older. A quiet boy, Peri; I didn't know much about him. All the others had been until yesterday our playmates, but Peri was always the bystander in our games and races.

'Three hours perhaps,' he said now. 'They're taking the goats to the upper pasture. They have the descent to make and the search party to assemble. They can't be here before mid-day.'

Cassie let out a high-pitched, excited wail. 'Oh, Cal, Cal, what are you going to do?'

'At least they are both unharmed,' said Athie. 'We were afraid for you,' she added, looking towards me.

'First we must bury the dead,' said Dio, getting to his feet. He startled the others into silence. We led the way. Everyone stood round the old man's body, staring. Lukas began to cry – as though he could know anything. Peri looked at the water-jug, the bracken bed, the blanket over the old man's body, and said, 'This is what you were doing all night . . .'

'But when they see this they will know . . . they will stop being angry,' said Athie.

'Perhaps,' said Peri.

'Snakes, you should have seen the fuss!' said Vryon. 'They were running around, not knowing what to do with the roast goat, and talking about looking for you in the dark, and the old women were yatter, yattering, and Cal's mother was crying, and Dio's lot were tucking their mouths up and looking as if they'd lost a drach and found a scorpion . . .'

'Shut up, Vryon, you're upsetting Cal,' said Niko, suddenly. It was true.

'We have to bury him,' said Dio. 'Now.'

'Even if we all help,' said Peri, 'It will take a while to make a hole in the marble fields.'

'He said what to do. There is a dry well somewhere, with a capstone. We are to put him down that.'

Athie said, 'Wouldn't it be better to leave him for the grown-ups to see when they come?'

'It wouldn't be decent,' Dio said.

And, indeed, with the rising light and flooding warmth of the morning, a cloud of flies was gathering round the body, and a sickly sweetness tainted the air in the makeshift shelter where he lay.

'Help us find the well,' said Dio, and the children scattered, Athie, borne down by Lukas, going last and slowest. I wasn't any use. I stumbled into a sunlit courtyard, sat down on a chunk of marble, and cried. I was tired, and over-excited, and wanting to run home to my mother. Vryon's talk of her in tears had wrenched my heart.

Athie came towards me, saying, 'Here, Cal, if you're just sitting there you could hold Lukas for me . . .' She held him out to me. Then she said, 'Why, you're sitting on it, aren't you?' I leapt up, and we both looked at the marble I had used as a chair. A round stone slab, on a drum-like platform. We whooped and called, summoning the others back to us. It took all the boys to roll the capstone off. We leant over the yawning hole beneath it. And it wasn't empty. Just below the rim was an iron bracket, fixed in the curving wall. Solid brickwork, the sort of thing they made in the Ago. Knotted to the bracket was a rope, not the kind of thing we make now, but bright blue, shiny, thick and tightly twisted. It ran down into the darkness, and just dimly visible down there was a grey mass of something, suspended.

Peri whistled. Cassie said, 'I don't like this,' and turned her back, walking away towards the broken wall of the court we were in, and picking poppies from among the stones. The poppies folded at once in the heat, and wilted across her hands. A breath of coldness stroked my face as I stared downwards, trying to make out the grey shape – an up-draught from the land of underground. It made me shiver.

Dio moved round to the point where the bracket was, shouldering the others out of the way, and took a hold on the blue rope. When he pulled, it came up easily. But the grey shape moved too. Something was suspended on the end of the rope, something bulky but not heavy, and Dio was hauling it up towards the light of day, hand over hand. The blue rope resisted coiling at his feet, having been tensed so long; it sank reluctantly into wide loops on the dusty flag-stones behind him.

And that grey bundle . . . it had a horrible resemblance to what we were about to replace it with. Coarse undyed linen, tied tightly round a tapering object with thin twine . . . a long object . . . We all stared at it, uneasy.

'This is what he meant,' said Dio. 'He just said we would find it. The treasure. He knew we would, if we buried him as he asked. Perhaps if we weren't going to bury him as he asked he didn't mind us not finding it . . .'

'What is it?' I said.

'I don't know,' said Dio. 'We must open it up.'

I was terrified. The image of a body tied tightly in a shroud which the thing presented, the grey dusty state of the wrappings, horrified me. I thought of what we find of a goat which the vultures have not cleaned for us . . .

And Dio I saw — I suppose I watched Dio with great intensity, my fate now hanging on him — was hesitating. He was stooped over the sinister object. He had drawn the knife from his belt to cut the thing open, but his hand froze for a long second, holding the knife-blade suspended over a length of twine pulled upwards in his other hand, and ready to snap at a touch.

Then Niko set up a cry of excitement; he had spotted something else, another something hanging on cord, on the opposite side of the well. We hadn't seen it so quickly, because it was on ordinary flaxen twine, the usual dull colour, and because it was smaller and had been hanging deeper, masked by the larger bundle.

Niko began to pull it upwards as he shouted. He was excited; he hauled it rapidly to the top, and was pulling so hard that the bundle flew over the rim and fell to the flagstones. It made a sound as of broken dishes as it fell. A bright fragment cut through the cloth wrapping, and shone like sunlit water.

'You fool, Niko!' cried Dio, straightening up. 'You've broken it!'

Niko began to cry. Athie and I sat down on the sun-baked stones, and began with little picking movements to extract the broken object from the cloth. We were afraid of cutting our fingers, but there were fewer broken edges than there might have been. We uncovered a glass bowl. A bowl made of a mirror – I knew it was mirror because my grandmother had a little piece of one she could look in to brush her hair, and although it was so small you could see more brightly in it than in any of the burnished metal ones the village craftsmen made. It was a big bowl, about thirty centimetres across, and nearly as much deep. When Niko dropped it it had broken into three parts, like jagged slices of watermelon: three curving glass shards. They lay bared on the ground, and shot blinding rays of the sun into our eyes, so that we could not look at them properly. We blinked, turned away our faces, and carried them into the shade.

'It doesn't have a stand. Or feet. Or a flat bottom to let it stand up,' said Athie, ever practical. 'It would make a terrible fruit-bowl.'

'A still worse wash-bowl,' said Cassie.

'It isn't a bowl!' I said, full of scorn. 'It's sacred; it's a . . . a thing.'

'I didn't mean to break it!' wailed Niko. 'It was an accident . . .'

'It's a shame,' said Peri, quietly. 'It was a lovely thing. A bowl for light. But it can't be helped. And stop crying, Niko; the gods, if they are taking any notice at all, will know that you didn't mean it.'

'We must hurry,' said Dio, and he leant down abruptly and cut the twine round the first bundle. It was another mystery he unwrapped. It was in a large piece of linen – a shroud. But it had nothing to do with death. An Ago thing if ever I saw one, as puzzling as the mirrored bowl, and just as beautiful. It was a cone, about three feet long, made of some metal, elaborately etched with a lovely flowing pattern. It was quite light. Dio picked it up, holding it at the point on the taper where the thickness sat nicely in his hand, and held it up high. We were pleased; it was somehow cheering to see Dio like that, waving the thing at the sky. He looked like a young pioneer from the Ago pictures on the wall of the village meeting-hall. Only a moment; then Dio lowered the thing and looked into the top of it. It was full of something. In the centre was a mecho of some kind, a ring of something in a metal case. Projecting from that was what looked remarkably like a lampwick. And the body of the cone was packed with a sky-blue substance, soft and solid like fat, covered in a clear wrapping.

'We must bury the old man first, and look at that later,' said Dio.

The boys took the piece of linen and brought the body on it, using it like a hammock. Then we tied it roughly round the corpse, and lifted him over the edge of the well. When we pushed and let him fall, we heard nothing back from the ground; neither a thump, nor a splash, but only silence, though we leant over, our heads tilted, our ears inclined to hear for many seconds.

'We didn't give him money for the ferryman,' said Cassie.

'I forgot,' said Dio, aghast.

'I've got some,' said Athie, 'Here. Safe journey!' and she threw a coin down the well. We heard it chink, and chink again, ricocheting more and more faintly.

'Let's go from here,' said Peri. 'We'll get the creeps.'

'What will you do with your treasures, Dio?' asked Vryon.

'I think we have no more time. I think I heard voices on the path,' I said. My hearing was sharpest; none of the others had anything to fear as I had. And I was right. We could hear voices clearly now. The party from the village was coming.

'Hide!' said Dio. We scattered, we ran in among the marbles and trees and rocks, and vanished from the courtyard of the well. Dio had picked up the cone treasure, and I picked up two pieces of the mirror treasure. I did not see who took the other one; only that when I looked back it too had gone, leaving only the wrappings and cords lying by the uncapped well.

The villagers trooped across the marble fields, calling. At first they called gently, naming us; then with anger. Lastly they too scattered and began to look for us. I permitted myself to feel scornful. All day they leave us free to wander. They give us the goats to keep, the goats which run everywhere and walk ledges less than a hand's breadth wide. I have seen a woman force her daughter along such a ledge at a deadly height to fetch down a kid; I have seen a terrified child forced at such risk, weeping, because of a kid that was a dinner, or a swap for a bowl of grain. And then they think they can find us on the hillsides, do they? These lumbering clumsy men and stout women think they can catch us even if they find us? I was curled up safely in a small patch of deep shadow behind a rock, within sight and sound of them, all the time they thought they had looked everywhere. My run to safety was just above me; one flying leap would have taken me behind a boulder and into the gully of a tiny stream, along which I would have gone in a flash had they seen where I was, but they didn't. My gloating and my scorn ended abruptly, when someone found Vryon. They dragged him into view, cuffed him on each ear in turn so that he fell to his knees, dazed and dizzy, and left him with two of the women. After that I was full of dread that they would find Dio. That I would be left alone. We knew, of course, exactly how long they had got before they would have to start back for the village on pain of being still on the paths in darkness. Time went by and Vryon was the only one they had found.

Then Niko's father brought him, squealing and fighting, held under one arm like a piglet, and dumped him down beside Vryon. Then in ones and two the searchers came back to base, gathered again around their two small prisoners.

Voices rose in a blur to my hiding-place; I couldn't hear what words. But Niko and Vryon were talking, answering questions. The men's voices droned on, conferring. Then Dio's father strode to the edge of the court and, facing the open hillside, raised his voice and called. 'Dio! Dio! Listen to me. Come out; let us take you home!' The hill was silent. Nothing stirred. 'Dio! Come out! We won't make you marry that girl, not now!' That was how I learnt that Dio too had been forced. Somehow I had assumed that at least he had wanted me, even if I didn't want him. But it had all been about those adjacent olive groves. I saw that now.

'Dio! Be reasonable! You can't be Guardian; that's all rubbish! We won't stand for it . . . humouring the old man was one thing, but that's at an end, you understand? You'll starve; and anyway we'll catch you sooner or later . . . Dio, can you hear me? Come home!'

I was full of fear that Dio would quietly stand up from behind a boulder, and come meekly down the slope to his father, and his supper, and the only life any of us knew . . . he didn't.

'I'll give the little beast such a leathering when I get hold of him!' said his father with sudden ferocity. I hoped Dio was near enough to hear that!

And then their time was up, and they were giving up, they were leaving in ones and twos, with Vryon gripped firmly by each hand between two of his grown brothers, and Niko carried on his father's back. And as they went, suddenly there was Athie coming between the scruffy trees on the marble fields to join them. She was carrying Lukas; what else could she do? We heard the women scold her, and the

20

relief in their voices. Someone took the baby from her arms. At that she made a movement as if to run, but one of the old women had hold of her firmly by a clutch of her clothes.

'Blessings and luck!' she called to us, and the stones glowing gold in the sinking sun shared her voice echoing round and round.

We gave them ten minutes on the homeward path, and then at last we came out of the shadows, and in the rapidly thickening dusk we went to find kindling for a fire to see us through the night. We had water; I thought we would have nothing to eat, but Cassie had brought a loaf when she set out that morning, supposing we might be hungry when the children found us, and so it was only fright that kept me wakeful the night long. Not at the animal sounds and scufflings, the creature noises of the place, or the stars nakedly blazing over our uncovered heads: but at what we had done, and would now have to do.

There was a clear and lovely dawn, made of a bitter lemon light. It cast at first shadows of a murky purple hue, so that when I woke and looked round, full of fear, at the others, they looked like the fallen statues of porphyry that lay on the great court of the marble fields a little distance off. I scrambled to my feet and gazed down at the others, sleeping. Cassie, bird-boned, thin-faced, a skinny child, her enormous eyes closed, but her mouth twitching slightly as she dreamed. Even at rest, her face and limbs suggested mobility. She was not one I would have chosen, too excitable, too easily crying and quarrelling, and singing a moment after an outburst of tears. Beside her at a little distance lay Peri, his dark and tousled head propped on one arm, face down, legs gracelessly sprawled. He looked strong, close-knit. But he was so quiet. I knew nothing about him, really. And Dio. Dio looked most of all like the men of porphyry. He was handsome; slender

21

and supple, and not yet beyond the physique of a boy. And his hair was full of light. The level beams of the morning reached his golden hair and blazed there. The shadows blackened and lost their lilac tone, and the whiteness of rising day woke Peri, and stopped my reverie.

One abrupt movement from Peri as he sat up, and the other two were also awake. It lay in my mind like lead that Athie was the strong and sensible one, and that she had chosen to go home.

'First we must cover the well,' said Dio.

But we could not lift the capstone. Four of us together could not lift it an inch, and the effort made us afraid of wrenched muscles, or of worse injury.

'We can't do this,' Peri said. 'But we might manage to use that slab.' He pointed to a large flagstone, not more than an inch or so thick, lying a few feet away, one corner lifted by the delicate velvet stems of an outburst of poppies.

And that we could lift and carry – just – all four of us together. When we laid it on the well it made a lid, though not an entire one. A broken corner left a chink of the darkness open to the light and air of day. But it was the best we could do.

We stood round, panting from the strain of heaving and lifting.

Peri looked up, towards the path. 'They will be coming back,' he said.

But Dio leant down and called through the chink in the stone, called to the other world like some mad old woman. 'Can you hear me?' he called. 'You! The Guardian before me, can you hear? I cannot keep the treasure the way you did; you must see that. But I will keep it the best way I can, I swear I will!'

A terrible dismay swept over me, as I heard and saw this. For Dio had become a mystery to me, as though he had been a child of another race, another time.

Three

We smelt burning. Cassie smelt it first, saw, let out a wail of dismay. A wisp of smoke was trailing in the light breeze of morning from behind a boulder at the edge of the court of the well. The grass was flaming, crackling.

'The bowl, the bowl!' Cassie cried, 'that's where we put the bowl!' And so it was. When we had beaten out the fire, flapped at it with hastily broken-off branches, and when Peri had dropped a piece of flagstone on the heart of it, and it was sulking away in dying sparks and charred entangled stems, we saw that a shard of the bowl was lying immediately beside it, dimmed with smoke.

'I've seen that trick before,' Peri said, 'or, at least, I've seen a fire lit accidentally like that. From a bit of a glass – Ago glass, clear as water.'

'How does it do it?' asked Dio, frowning.

'I don't know how,' he said, looking at Dio confidingly, and despairingly. 'You know Dio, we don't know *anything* any more. But it works. It can burn your hand.'

'Show me,' Dio said.

Peri picked up a clean piece of the bowl, and held it towards the sun. The sun was still low, shining at a shallow angle. He made a bright point of light by tipping the bowl till its reflection lay like a tiny bright coin in the slab we had laid on the well. 'Put your hand there, if you're fool enough,' he said.

Dio snatched his hand away almost at once, wincing, looking with amazement at the little pink hurt blushing up on his knuckle. Then of course each of us had to try it.

'The sun is teaching us,' Dio said. 'I see now. I see what the old man was telling us – what these two things have to do with each other. This cone is a torch; it needs to be lit. The bowl does that. I see. So listen to me now. I have to save the torch. Ago, people came to fetch it. They came every four years. It was important to them. But they must have forgotten where it is; they haven't come for many years – for more than a lifetime, perhaps. We shall light it now; it has to be lit by the sun here, at this place of stones and broken things. Then I shall take it and go with it, and find the people who wanted it. It is all I can think of to do.'

'Yes,' I said. I couldn't think of anything else he could do either, unless he just wanted to go home. Just the same, I thought he was talking very strangely. It crossed my mind to wonder if he was light-headed from hunger.

'Cal has to come with me,' Dio went on, 'because she is probably my wife. And if she is not my wife, she had still better come with me. But you two can choose.'

'Let's see if it works, first,' I said.

'Oh, it will work all right,' said Cassie, suddenly. I stared at her. How odd of her to think she knew. But then, Cassie was a bit odd. She used to sit down beside flowers and lizards, and tell them stories.

And then it didn't work. We tipped the glass pieces this way and that, and we shone the burning discs they threw on the wick of the torch, and on the mecho bit, and on some of the blue stuff, and nothing worked.

Our time was running out. Surely the village elders would come back to look for us again – more of them this time, probably.

'It must be because it's broken,' said Dio, at last. 'Can't we mend it?'

'I don't think that stuff mends,' said Peri, shaking his head.

'But what if we held the pieces together, as though they weren't broken at all? What then?' said Cassie.

It took three of us, six handed, to hold the three heavy, slippery bits of glass back in a bowl shape. We tried to tilt it to the sun, and it slid apart. In the end we were standing like three columns, holding it up, our hands like the sepals of a flower on the cup of its petals. Dio sprang up on the well and plunged the torch upside down into the bowl, cool on our hands, and incandescently bright within.

And the torch leapt into flame.

As it did so we heard the clatter of running feet on the path.

'Come, if you are coming,' Dio said, and he took a step or two, torch in hand.

'Where?' I asked.

'We must escape,' he said. 'We must go by the goat tracks towards Lalas, and northwards through the mountains.'

'There's a path they won't know,' Cassie said. 'I'll show you.' She led the way to the edge of the marble fields, at a point just to the side of the track from home. She walked between bushes and boulders, and then abruptly moved out of sight. At that moment the expected sound of footfalls on the path from the village reached me. There was a moment when I held back. I was alone between the figures of Dio and Peri, picking their way ahead, following Cassie, and the sound of pursuit. There was a moment when the choice was made, but I did not seem to do the choosing. I was not Guardian. I was not Dio's wife. If I liked I could have said it was all nothing to do with me. But I too skipped between the bushes, and followed on.

Cassie's route, around the foot of the hill and across a scrubby meadow, led to the bank of the river Cladeus, trickling down its rocky bed. It had once been more of a river, and still flooded in the spring, but now it was a small flow of water in a wide band of boulder and gravel bank. There were ready hiding-places along it, in among the bushes that clustered in hope of moisture, and the hollows of its overhanging dry banks, and following it we ascended gently mile by mile. It led us, in quite a short time, on to a goat track, fairly easy going, trailing off at a gentle rise towards the distant mountains. Once we gained this path it was easy walking with occasional scrambles over screes, but it left, almost at once, the last few yards of the territory of our village; and so it felt strange and perilous. People, in my recollection, never left the village, or if they did they never came back. I felt abruptly foolish. I was always asking questions; I had spent the first thirteen years of my life asking, asking, till I got cuffed for it; yet I had never asked about outside the village and its lands, never really wondered about it at all. Only in dreams had I left it, and now, naturally, I felt as though I were dreaming, trailing along behind a boy bridegroom with a torch thing shining in his right hand. The torch had died down quite a bit from the leaping flames with which it had taken fire in the mirrored bowl; it burned now with a small steady flame like a candle, quite clean and smokeless. But it was bright enough to be seen for miles and miles; a beacon to anyone coming after us. Nobody could be coming after us; whoever it was we had heard on the path, just before we had taken Cassie's track away from there, would have needed hours to pick up our trail again. They would be far behind. And yet . . . I was walking last. There should have been no sound of footfalls behind me, no startled bird flying up from a bush now far behind . . . I told myself uneasily that I did not know what a valley, a hillside, would be like when there was nobody in it. The creatures would go their own ways, make their sounds . . .

We came out on higher ground, and now we could see the heights of Rimanthos ahead of us, radiant under their faint sunlit snows. We took a crooked way, going on goat tracks, doubling back and redoubling. We avoided well-beaten paths, though we crossed a number of them, keeping away from villages. The sun was high above our heads before we stopped. The others had found a little spring of fresh water and a big boulder casting shade. We drank, and rested, and tried not to think of food. And all the time I kept an uneasy eye on the path behind us. I couldn't get rid of the feeling that we were being followed, though how any search party had contrived to keep on the track I couldn't think. Peri and Cassie were still sleeping, and the torch, propped in a bush, was burning faintly, barely visible in the brilliant light of full day, when Dio came quietly up behind me and put a hand on my shoulder. 'What's worrying you?' he said. 'You're watchful, jumpy.'

'Someone coming after us. Perhaps.'

'What makes you think?'

'It's just a feeling.' But as I spoke we both saw, far behind us, a movement. A speck of colour, crossing between a rock and a bush; just a glimpse, and it was gone. We strained our eyes. We would have liked to see how many they were, and how fast they were going. But we couldn't pick out anything else, or even, after a few moments of riveted staring at the sun-blurred distance, be sure exactly where the path lay, or where to go on looking.

But Dio had seen it too. He woke the others, and we conferred. Peri was for going over the mountain, instead of below it. 'They won't think of that,' he said. I stared up at the looming shadowy mass of Rimanthos, wearing its spring cloak of white. No, of course they wouldn't think of it. The boys decided. We started off again, this time leaving the path abruptly, and striking directly towards the shining caps of snow that cloaked the peaks above the paths and passes. When, climbing slowly and doggedly, we reached the lower edges of the snow, there were fierce springs of melt-water and fringes of icicles, the ground was sodden, and the snow soft, wet and treacherous. As we crossed the margins we were soaked to the skin, and we slowed down to a crawling pace, struggling and slipping; suddenly we were short of breath and shivering. I began to falter and stop.

'Keep up,' Dio told me. 'We won't wait for you. And if we lose you you'll die.'

His harshness stung me, but I nodded, and struggled on.

At the top of a nasty scramble up a shining, glass-clear waterfall of re-frozen thaw, I stopped for breath. And as soon as I stopped I was in trouble, trembling and shaking, and finding breathing harder than ever. 'Keep moving!' Peri called to me. 'Keep moving or you'll freeze in no time!' But when we reached the crest of the shoulder we were climbing and looked down to the other side, the sun was dropping down the sky away to our left, and the path was far below us, further, I thought than we could go by nightfall. We would freeze anyway.

'What are we doing up here?' I asked.

'It's five hours on the path, and three this way,' Dio said. 'We're putting two hours between ourselves and the pursuit.'

'We're putting eternity between, more like,' I said.

'No,' said Dio. 'Not yet. We'll get down as far as we can, and then camp somehow.'

We had longer than I had thought, because the downward slope faced the setting sun. A golden sheen burnished the perilous slopes of ice, and turned slowly rosy as we slipped and scrambled down. We all fell, over and over again, and Cassie fell and slipped so far that I was sure she would fall into a crevasse and we would lose her. She stopped herself in the end, clawing at the watery glaze on the snows, lying full-length in a thrusting spout of melt-water, her feet wedged on the first bare rock we had seen this side of the pass.

The sun was losing itself across the lowlands beyond, the mountainside was turning crimson, and the shadows were the colour of blood. We pulled Cassie out of the stream, and took it in turns to hold her tight, trying to share what warmth we had. But we were all wet through and chilled to the marrow.

Peri seemed to know what we needed. He set Dio to scraping now and finding bits of the dead, woody stems of herbs beneath. All along the edge of the bitter stream he found stuff, sodden every bit of it, and brought it. He was working in a deep drift, hollowing out a shallow cave. In a little Cassie recovered enough to help, and I worked at scooping the snow in my hands and throwing it into a heap a few feet in front of the cavity. It looked not big enough for a goat, but somehow Peri got all four of us into it, pressed tightly together, and out of the flow of freezing air that made us suffer so. Dio used the torch to light our damp sticks. It took a while to work, but then it blazed up brightly for a little. Dio planted the torch for safety in the mound of snow I had built across the mouth of the shelter. We lay like a litter of puppies, our hands and feet hurting horribly, and watched.

I hadn't seen the torch close to before. I had thought it was like a lamp; but now it seemed more like a brazier. It glowed a dark red, and gave out heat long after our pitiful fire had hissed out in a pool of water. It saw us through the night.

I thought I was not sleeping; I was on the outside of the huddle of limbs, and I thought I was waking while I froze to death; but I must have slept, for the dawn light woke me. Woke us, rather, for we all stirred together, our interlaced bodies reacting as one. Stiff and aching we stood up, and looked at the softly glowing valley below us. We stretched out our raw and swollen hands to the faint warmth of the torch, and stamped our numb feet.

'Down off the snow as fast as we can,' said Dio.

And as he spoke there came a sound from behind us, from far above us, on the way we had come. A sharp sound: a dog barking.

'Oh, but they couldn't have!' cried Cassie. 'Surely they wouldn't . . . they wouldn't have done that!' Her voice was terrified. And my heart seemed to have jumped into the back of my mouth, and was beating there, choking me. The dogs were for death-hunts. For catching raiders and bandits who would otherwise prey on the village, for tearing them limb from limb. We all began to run, blundering, stumbling, our limbs still locked with cold.

The distant barking intensified; it was already nearer than before. I went on running and falling for quite a while before it penetrated my frozen wits that it was only one dog; one dog barking hysterically, not a pack. High-pitched, not the booming baying of the hunt.

'Wait! Stop!' I called. And our stampede slowed down, we caught hold of rock and bushes, and Cassie, who had been bouncing and sliding down the slopes on her bottom, gingerly stood up.

Just one dog was running after us. A small black one. The moment we stopped and let her gain ground on us we knew it was Mela, a black mongrel bitch. Niko's dog. She whimpered and grovelled as she reached us. She cowered to the ground, her tail wagging. She made whining and crying sounds. Dio bent and scratched behind her ears. 'All right, old girl, all right,' he said. 'You can come with us. All right . . .'

But when he took a step downward she suddenly snarled,

and sank her teeth into his sleeve, and tugged. He shook her off easily. 'Let's go,' he said. 'We are losing the hours we gained.' Mela flew at me, and bit my skirts, and pulled. She sat down on her haunches with her teeth locked in my clothes, and snarled.

We got the message. 'She wants us to go back . . .' I said.

'Niko!' said Cassie. The moment we stepped her way, Mela let go and ran ahead of us, climbing back up the wastes of dripping ice and impacted snow. It took us a good half hour to climb back to our overnight ice-hole. Some hundred feet above that the dog led us to a screen of icicles, hanging over an arching snowdrift, hollowed by partial thaw. There, out of sight, lay Niko, tightly curled and with his hands tucked into his sheepskin jacket, and his face blue and faintly transparent, like the ice-screen behind which he lay. Mela nudged at him with her nose, whimpered, put out a sudden, lolloping pink tongue, and licked him. Then she lay down alongside him, and looked at us.

'It was *Niko* following us!' said Dio.

'Is he dead, Peri?' I said in a whisper.

'Looks it,' he replied. I could feel the faintest line of warmth on my deadened cheeks, as tears flowed. I thought they would freeze as they ran. Poor Niko . . . But he wasn't stiff. When we picked him up and began to carry him, he lay slack and heavy in Peri's arms.

Once more we began the scrambling, sliding descent, full of bruising falls. Peri couldn't carry Niko all the way; Cassie and I, taking him between us, took one or two turns. We were so cold, so frozen-witted, it took some time for us to realize that if it was Niko who had been following us, then there was no more danger, no more need for speed and flight. We could take our time, choose our footing, pay heed to avoiding falls. It must have been nearly mid-day when at last we reached the zone of rushing water, the spouting

31

melt-streams, and the sodden, snow-burnt brown herbs of the hillside underfoot. Mud and stones instead of ice lay before us, and an obvious hill-path, leading down. Mela padded along in front of us, nose down, circling back now and then to run at the heels of whoever had Niko at the time. I liked to see her, trotting along ahead.

Then there were terraces, with olive trees. Even a little whitewashed summerhouse, with a donkey manger on the wall. At last there was a pantiled dome and a cluster of houses in view ahead, and the path turned twice abruptly on the hillside and led into the village. Mela stopped, and growled.

But what could we do? Even if they killed us; even if they tied our hands and took us back home for punishment, they were our only alternative to death from hunger and cold. Dio held the torch firmly and took the lead, and we stumbled round the last turn of the path and into a narrow street.

Four

We were afraid; as we would have been if it had been our own village we were entering, returning. In a thousand years I would not have guessed what would happen. The first few folk who saw us murmured, and ran into their houses; few strangers ever came to them, I thought, as few as to us at home. But then they ran out of their doors again, with all their kinsfolk, so that suddenly the little lane was crowded with a surge of people, young and old, calling, 'The torch! The torch has come again!' They trooped after us in a buzz of excited voices, laughing, shouting. Some ran ahead, crying out, banging on doors as they helter-skeltered past. So that when in a few yards we reached the centre of the place, a little square with a broken-down fountain in it, it was full of a thronging crowd.

We stopped, uncertain, and stood close together, waiting. They were bringing somebody, somebody so old and venerable he could not walk or stand, but was brought out in a wooden chair, and set down on the steps of the church. We faced him. The buzz of voices hushed a bit. The old man had watery eyes, bloodshot and clouded as though with a drop of milk in water. He trembled, hand and foot. His beard and hair were like strands of gossamer, and his skull was nearly naked. A little trickle of spittle ran down his chin. When he spoke I jumped, for his voice, though it creaked, was steady and loud. 'Where are the Games?' he said.

'I don't know that,' said Dio.

33

An indrawn breath moved the crowd like a gust of wind. I knew that Dio had made the wrong answer.

'So, you are not the runner,' said the elder.

'I thought not,' a woman said, from our right somewhere. 'He doesn't look like a runner.'

'You have stolen the torch,' said the elder.

'No,' said Dio. I was amazed at how calm he sounded. Fear and hunger and weariness were eating at me. 'I have not stolen it, but I am not the runner. I am the new Guardian.'

The old man shook his head. 'The Guardian doesn't come. The runner comes. The Guardian waits. Why is there a new Guardian?'

'The old Guardian is dead,' said Dio. 'He gave me his title, and showed me where the things were hidden, and it was not safe to wait. They told me I could not be Guardian. So we lit the torch and brought it across the mountain to find what it is for.'

An elderly woman standing just behind the elder's chair leaned forward and said to him softly, 'Could they have lit it if they had stolen it?'

'Perhaps not,' the elder said. He stared at us. 'They are savages at Olim nowadays. I don't know about what you are doing. It may be the right thing, it may be wrong. Where did you light the torch?'

'On the marble fields, with a magic bowl,' Dio said. The old man nodded. 'That much was right,' he said. 'Well, I see that you are not going anywhere unless we feed and warm you. One of you seems to be dead already.'

'We need help,' said Dio.

'It is a sacred thing you carry,' the elder said. 'We will help you.' He made a tremulous gesture to the young men who had carried him to meet us. 'A fire,' he said. 'Clothes, and food. The torch is come again, as I never thought to see

34

it, and the torch-bearers are our bounden duty and ancient charge.'

Someone took Niko from my aching arms, and we were led across the square, through the press of people, and into a house.

They were kind. A huge bronze bowl of charcoal burned in the middle of the room, and they brought sheepskins for us to sit on close around it. Niko was laid out gently on a pallet some way from the fire, and covered in rugs. The women warmed blankets at the brazier and laid them over him, changing them and rewarming them constantly. They brought us soup, and warned us not to gulp it, but to go slowly, slowly. They would not let us hold out our hands to the heat; that too was to take time. They told us the snow-sickness was upon us, and we must do as we were told. And the moment we were warmed through, and full of bowls of soup, we were overcome with sleepiness, nodding and drowsing, and unable to hold up our heads. They carried us to side aisles, laid us out on sheepskin beds, and spoke kindly to us, though we were beyond understanding the murmuring voices around us. I woke when they laid me down; surfacing like a swimmer about to sink again. One of the women stroked the hair back from my forehead – a touch like my mother's touch. And I heard Niko's voice, suddenly piercing, 'You were too hard to catch!' he cried. 'You might have waited . . .'

But in the moment of leaping joy that his living voice brought to me, I was engulfed in sleep.

I woke late; the fires were out, the doors of the house open to the street. Somewhere in the back yard a woman was softly singing. And outside there was a murmur of voices, low, continuing. Bread and a pitcher of milk stood on the hearthstone, gently warmed by the dying embers. I got

35

up, and began to eat. Niko, I saw, was lying curled, covered, and drowsing still. The others had all woken and left their bedshelf. On mine, I saw, as I squatted, swigging the thickly creamy milk, a clean coarse woollen longshirt lay ready, with my own belt. I put it on, and went out. The cold air of morning scoured my lungs, and the bright light struck me in the face, and stung me into alertness as I stepped across the threshold. The voices were from a conference in the street.

The elder was sitting in his chair, under the portico of the church. The church steps had carpets spread upon them, and a throng of young people were sitting round, with Dio in the midst and Cassie close beside him. I held back a moment or two, watching. Women crossing the square stopped and listened, and passed on; people joined or left the circle as they pleased. Then Dio saw me and beckoned. 'Come and hear this,' he said. 'You will help me remember.'

A silken rug in colours of faded red and gold was spread for me, and I sat down and listened. And the elder began to tell us a wonderful story, and one we had never heard before.

In times long, long past, he said, many years before the time we called Ago, was a time called 'Antiquity'. And in those times, longer back than we could dream of, we, the Hellenes, had been the richest people in the world. But our wealth had been not like the fabled wealth of Ago, not in mechos and in singing boxes and flying carts and suchlike, but in the beauty of the thoughts of the people, and what they made with their heads and hands. They were without shame, these ancestors of ours, and would run and wrestle and jump and throw things, standing naked, making themselves beautiful and strong to please their gods. For these Games they made the marble fields, only they were not fields then, full of fallen fragments, but level grounds, terraces for onlookers, seats for judges, columns and halls

36

and rooms and temples, and baths . . . there were many such places but the greatest of all was at Olim.

'What happened?' asked Cassie. 'What went wrong?'

'I don't know that,' the elder said. 'The story does not say. But it says the Hellenes were always fighting among themselves. War raged in their tiny valleys, each town and village against others. So that the Games and the races would not take place without a truce; and time after time they made a truce for them. Then the young men and women would go to Olim, and compete for a prize.'

'What was the prize, Grandad?' said a piping child from the front of the crowd of listeners.

We smiled at a childish question. 'That's a curious thing,' the elder said, very seriously. 'The prize was nothing; nothing of worth at all. A crown of leaves that faded in a day, and a small jar of oil. A few drachs would have bought it . . .'

How strange, I thought. A strangeness that made my scalp prickle, as when I thought I had seen a ghost.

'A thousand years went by,' the elder said, 'before the Games at Olim faded away. But at last they ceased, though not the memory of them. A thousand years of Games, each four years, then more than a thousand years without them. And then the world was in the time we call Ago. A great chieftain arose, whose title was Baron. He began the Games again, but this time not at Olim. By now we were poor farmers, of little account, we folk of Hellada. The Games were held in places important in the times called Ago. But they brought the fire from Olim to them wherever they were, as a sign.'

'As a sign of what?' said Dio, softly.

'The story does not say that. It says, "as a sign". That is all. I am telling only what was handed down to me, Guardian. Doubtless there was once more. Once the stories made sense,

37

and those who told them understood them. But we are fallen into this state of confusion now. Long since, I think.'

He paused, shaking his head, so that I was afraid Dio's words had stopped him. A young woman jumped up from the group of us, and brought him a cup of water from the fountain. He sipped, and sighed.

'In the Ago time,' he went on, 'cunning craftsmen made many torches, ready for the years to come. They left them at Olim, and the people of Olim set a Guardian upon them to keep them safe. Then the glory of Ago faded away, and we lost the cunning and the riches, and the Games were skipped, and interrupted, and held seldom. The torches were used up, one by one, and then when no runner had come for years the temple was raided, and some of the remaining torches were stolen and burned at wedding feasts in the south. Then the last Guardian hid the one last torch, and the mirrored bowl to catch the golden light at Olim, and stayed on the ruined stadium day and night. And now that too is over, and the last torch is lit and on its way . . .'

'We have done the wrong thing,' I said. 'We did not know enough. We must put out the torch and put it back where we found it.'

'No,' said Dio, confident and clear. 'Somewhere in the world there are Games again, and in our hearts we were told to take the flame, and find them.'

'In any case,' the elder said, 'I have been told that, once lit, the torches cannot be re-lit. If they go out, all is lost. The Ago men who made them wanted to be sure it was one and the same flame lit at Olim which reached the start of the Games, not something lit and quenched and lit at will, like a watchman's lamp.'

'So now the last torch is burning . . .'

'You have, while it lasts, to find a place for it.'

'How long will it last?'

38

'I do not know. I have seen a torch go from Olim, when I was a young child. But I have never heard of anyone returning who went with it.'

Dio said, 'You are old, and you know a lot. We are only untaught children from the goat-runs across the mountain. Tell us what you think we should do.'

The elder shook his head. 'The journey of the torch is your doing, Dio from Olim, not mine. I don't know what you should do. But we have decided to help you. We will give you food, and an escort on your way. And our Nikathlon will go with you. But it is all your doing.'

'Yes,' said Dio. 'Thank you. What is a Nikathlon?'

Five

'I am,' a boy said, stepping forward.

'Show them,' said the elder. The little boys ran to make ready for him, to set the jump for him at the far end of the square, to bring a straw-bale for the landing. People came flocking to watch; it was more interesting than the interminable talk of the morning. The boy was bent double, swaying on the balls of his feet, gathering the tension in his limbs, ready, ready . . .

'The mark is too high!' said Dio. 'He will hurt himself.'

The elder smiled.

Someone cracked a whip for the boy, and he released his strength. He ran like the wind, and leapt into the air, going like a diver over the mark, arching himself, falling head forward, and curling as he hit the straw, to roll safely in it, not to hit directly as he fell. We had heard the soft whistle of the air around the rod as his flight fanned it; he had seemed just to touch the rod as he went over, but when we looked up the rod was vibrating, but still in place. The people were all clapping, we were all staring at him, stupefied. He went and sat quietly down again, among the elder's household. He did not preen himself, or swagger. He looked remote – bored, even. The elder made him demonstrate running and throwing javelins, though, before he could rest.

'This is our Nikathlon,' the elder said. 'If you find Games, he can compete in them. He has beaten everyone else here at all of them since he was ten or so; now nobody will run or jump or throw here. Our youngsters play dice, and grow soft. He should go with you; a chance for him, and a chance for others.'

'But not unless he freely chooses,' said Dio. The boy looked up at that, startled; perhaps nobody ever argued with the elder.

'You are fantastic,' said Dio, going to stand in front of him. 'It would be good if you came. If you wanted to come. Do you want to?'

'My father has a small farm, and I have many brothers,' he said.

'So?' said Dio.

'And there is no one here to run against,' the boy added.

Dio nodded. 'But could any of us run against you, Nikathlon?' he said.

The boy got up and stared at us, looking us over one by one.

'You are good-looking enough, Torch-bearer,' he said, 'but not a runner, I think.' To Peri he said, 'You are made for wrestling, not for running or jumping . . .' He barely glanced at Niko, who was still pale, and shaky on his feet, or at Cassie, but he said to Dio, pointing at me, 'It might be worth training her. She could run.'

'I couldn't!' I said, hating him. 'Why do you say that? I can't run a step!'

'You are long and straight,' he said, 'with breasts like cobnuts, and an arse like a boy's. I would like to see you run . . .'

'You can whistle for that!' I said, embarrassed and indignant.

They gave us a good send-off. They were not rich people, just villagers, after all. But they gathered, and roasted a goat or two, and fed us as though we had been born there, and talked over the question of Games. They had never heard of any anywhere near there, now or ever, it appeared. But that evening there was a wandering leather-worker in the village, a man who mended harness and moved on when the work was done, and he said he thought there were summer Games in the Islands. He thought he had heard of Games at Palcastra, though he had only heard, and could not say for certain.

They lent donkeys, and even a pony for Dio, so that the torch could go with dignity. Of course, if we were going to Palcastra these were only lent; they would be left on the shore, and could be led back to the village. Poor Niko did not realize what that meant for Mela. But the brightly coloured swathes of cloth to make a good new cloak for each traveller, and the gifts of food and wine, and the leather water-bottle, and the little golden trinkets with coloured beads which were given to Dio as gifts for strangers along the way, all these were truly given, in true goodwill. From such a poor place these were princely gifts, and once up on his pony Dio made a halting speech of thanks, finishing with a hope that something might reward the elder and his villagers, for we had nothing to give but thanks.

'My son,' said the elder, 'it is true that men and women do many things in hope of return. But not all. Some things in life we do just because we think it good to do them. You are bearing the torch because you are bearing the torch. We are helping you go because we are helping you go. And farewell so.'

Then we trotted out of town, with a bevy of youngsters running behind us on foot, and a guide – the Nikathlon's uncle Michael, whom the elder used for messages and trading, we were told, and who knew the route to the shore. At the crest of the path, where it turned round the shoulder of the hillside and the village swung out of sight, Dio pulled up his pony, and for a moment or two looked back, while Niko, riding beside him, waved as though someone below might have been watching us out of sight.

'Don't you want to wave goodbye, Nikathlon?' Niko sang out.

But he did not pause or stop, or turn his head. He did not look back. 'There was nobody back there who could pace me, never mind beat me in a race,' he said.

Michael led us for three days. We were always descending; crossing ever more fertile and more level ground. We came to meadows, with cattle instead of goats, and with wheat growing in patches below large wide-spreading olives, and here and there plots of tobacco. Our village, we realized, was poor, having nothing but stumpy shrubs for trees, and stones for fields. No wonder there were more people down here on the plains. They were friendly; they were impressed enough by the sight of the shining torch, though very few of them, we gathered, knew anything about it. The stories about it had not spread very far around the mountains. But people knew Michael, and when we needed fodder for our mounts, or clean water, or a little food, he paid for it. We met no trouble.

So in three days we came down to a shore. There was a rocky inlet, a beach of pale pebbles, a row of boats hauled up on it, and nets spread about, drying. Michael paid our passage, the boatmen fetched a crew of oarsmen, and we dismounted on the stones of the beach and scrambled into the boat. Behind us the bevy of donkey-boys mounted in our places the unburdened animals, ready to ride them home, and called and waved to us. Dio sat down amidships, nursing the torch.

And Mela, of course, set up a fuss; she ran up and down at the water's edge, whimpering and barking.

'How is Mela getting on board?' asked Niko.

'Sorry, my friend, she is not,' said Michael. 'The boatmen won't take a dog; bad luck.'

'Then I'm not going either!' cried Niko. 'Let me off, let

me off!' But the boat was already drawing gently away from the beach.

Mela howled with grief, and Niko began to climb over the gunwale. Michael seized him, and covered him with his cloak. 'Listen,' he said. 'When she cannot see you she will cry no longer.' And indeed Mela fell silent almost at once, and when Michael let Niko peek from under the cloak, she was running along behind the donkey-train, leaving the beach.

'What will happen to her?' Niko said, sitting down again, with tears running down his cheeks.

'Is she a good farm-dog?' said Michael.

'She's a good ratter,' said Niko.

'I'll find a home for her when I get back, then,' said Michael.

All day long the oarsmen rowed us. A boy beat time on a drumskin, and they pulled, and sweated in the sun. We talked to them, smiled. Yes, the coxswain told us, there were Games at Palcastra. Peri even took an oar for a while. But the Nikathlon sat in the stern of the boat and watched, impassive. The water around us was calm and quiet. A light wind filled a red sail that the ganger hauled up the mast when we were well out to sea, but still they rowed, less urgently, sharing the work with the sail. A steep purple shadow stood up behind the horizon, and grew taller by degrees as we moved towards it. The oarsmen named it. 'Corfoo,' they said. 'Palcastra . . .' They waved their hands. When I saw how far it was I wondered what Michael had paid the boatmen, and what would be done without by the villagers in order to find our fares. But perhaps the elder had private treasure to pay for fancies such as this.

We sailed round the southern end of the great island, and making about began to move up the lee shore. The sail flapped idly, and the water died down to a glassy flatness, and took on a lilac and indigo shimmer in the evening light. The brightly coloured cloaks we wore glowed in the rosy air. The ganger ran down the sail, and the men began to row again, steadily, their dipping oars leaving shining rings behind, the ruby droplets falling as they glided forwards on the quiet thrust dropping a line of smaller ripples till the blades cut in again, and the plashing of the fierce pull in the soft water resumed.

The others watched the island shore; I, full of dislike, watched the Nikathlon; he watched the work, for, as the day stretched out and our rough-looking oarsmen still worked steadily, barely resting, never breathless, he had become interested in them. He was watching intently the pull of their contracting leg and arm muscles, the movement of stress rippling under the brown skin of their naked backs, the pivoting pressure of their feet on the benches in front of them.

The land loomed up high above us, and suddenly they all raised their oars in the rests, and let the boat run abruptly aground on a beach. We children all clambered through the shallows, and a pile of bundles was unloaded with us, and set upon the sands.

Michael spoke to Dio, and said 'Palcastra . . .', drawing a map on the sand. And then all the adults were in the boat, and the boat was pulling gently off the beach. The bank of oars seen from the shore looked like the wings of some waterfowl, sweeping rhythmically. The boat stood off and left us, fading into the deepening darkness, black against the setting sun, and we were left standing with no light but the bright flicker of the torch, and no sound but the sighing of the calm water in small waves at our feet.

We looked for driftwood to make a fire. It took some finding. The Nikathlon sat down, and listened to the lapping

45

water. I found Niko struggling with a hunk of driftwood, trying to drag it along.

'Not you, Niko,' I said. 'You're only just on your feet. You need to keep your strength. You gave us such a fright!'

'I couldn't catch up with you,' he said. 'You went so fast. I got there quite soon in the morning; you had only just gone. But I couldn't catch up. And then your tracks went in the snow . . .'

'I know. We thought you were the grown-ups coming after us. We were trying to shake you off. Poor Niko . . . no, put that down, it's heavy.'

I marched across to the Nikathlon. 'Come and help me lift a log,' I asked him. 'It's heavy.'

'I can't do that,' he said.

'Why not?'

'I might pull a muscle. Then where would I be?'

'Well, where would you be then? The same as any of us. Come and help.'

'No. I'm the Nikathlon; I don't do things, I only run. And I can't afford to hurt myself; just a little injury that wouldn't harm another person can make the difference between win and lose to me.'

'You're crazy,' I said. 'What does running matter?'

'What does anything else matter? You could do it too. I'll show you, if you like. You could train to pace me . . .'

'No thank you,' I said.

'You would be good at it,' he persisted.

'I'd rather not if it makes people pig-selfish like you,' I said.

He jumped up and would have hit me, I think, if I hadn't dodged him quickly in the dark. But I yelled as though he had hit me, and at once Dio and Peri arrived.

'What's up?' said Dio.

46

'The Nikathlon won't help me bring a log,' I said. 'He's just sitting there while everyone else works. In case he pulls a muscle.'

'Go with her and help,' said Dio. 'There aren't any privileges among us.'

'There are now,' the Nikathlon said coldly. 'There are mine. I don't do anything that might pull muscles, or tire me out.'

'Let's get it straight,' said Peri quietly, his hand on Dio's arm. The darkness was total now, and the torch was planted on the beach behind them, throwing their faces into shadow. 'You are saying that you will sit round the fire we have lit, and eat the food we have cooked, and walk with us, and share our welcome, and never lift a finger to help with anything? In case you hurt your precious self in some way? Is that what you are saying?'

'So that I can run unimpaired. Like a god. That's what it means to be Nikathlon.'

'No wonder they were so keen to be rid of him,' said Peri, snorting.

'No!' he said, furious. 'They were proud of me. I am the glory of the village . . .'

'Well, they didn't seem to mind losing you,' I said, 'and now we know why.'

'It is simple, Nikathlon,' said Dio. 'You will have your share of food when it is ready, because what we have now was given by your people. But either you will help us build a fire or you will not sit at it. As you like.'

The Nikathlon sat down at once upon the beach, scorning to reply.

We made ourselves comfortable, lighting a driftwood fire, and warming rounds of bread, full of lumps of cheese. Niko took the Nikathlon his share. 'Aren't you cold, Nikathlon,' we heard him ask, 'sitting out here by yourself? Dio would let you come and warm yourself if you say you will help tomorrow . . .'

Niko got no reply. And of course we all felt angry, uncomfortable in the kindly warmth of the fire, because of him, sitting sulking in the darkness. He was going to be horribly cold if he slept away from the fire all night.

When I had eaten, I got up and went over to him, hoping to mend matters somehow. And he had gone; taken his own bundle, and gone. I began to look for him, away from the fire, all along the darkened shore. At the end of the beach was a rocky headland, and as I reached it I stopped and turned. I could hear no sound of anyone moving, far or near – but he ran with such light footfalls! And I could see almost nothing but the two sparks of fire on the shore far behind.

And just then the moon swam up behind the headland, and showed me in the dimness a track leading inshore, and upward. It must go to a village or a town, or at least a farm. So I ran on.

The path led me round the shoulder of a steep headland, and then turned abruptly downhill and inland. It met a rocky, tumbling water, and crossed it over a simple bridge, little more than a tree trunk laid over the torrent. I padded over it, dryshod. Soon the path was wider, joined by tracks from left and right, and I saw ahead of me a city gate, with lanterns burning, and a fire in an iron basket glowing to keep the watchmen warm.

Outlined against the lanterns I saw the Nikathlon ahead of me, running steadily towards the gate. I was appalled at him, going alone into a strange city. What if they hated strangers? But before he quite reached them, I heard them call out to him.

'Some leave it late!' the watchman said. 'All the others have washed and eaten, and are safely asleep by now.'

'I have come from the mainland,' he said, 'and the ignorant seamen put me down on the wrong beach.'

'Never mind, lad,' said another of the guards, sounding fatherly. 'We'll give you a bite of supper, and you can slip into the stadium and find a bunk to sleep on. There are so many athletes here they won't notice when you arrived, shouldn't wonder.'

I skipped from shadow to shadow, and crouched behind a jut of the wall, listening, full of rage. 'You've missed the horse ride,' a guard was saying, ladling a bowlful of soup for the Nikathlon, and dropping into it a good hunk of coarse bread. 'But the heat for the running race is tomorrow. You must put your name on a scrap of paper or broken pot and drop it in the big jar by the arena gate. Don't be overcome; most of the other youngsters don't know what to do till someone tells them, any more than what you do.'

'Thank you,' said the Nikathlon. 'If I win the great race, I will reward you for your kindness.'

At which they all laughed, loudly and rudely, nudging each other in the ribs and gasping with mirth. I could not see what was funny; but obviously something was.

'Bet you won't, though!' said the foreman, at last. I would have loved to see the Nikathlon's face – he didn't like being laughed at.

'Give over, and tell him where to go,' said the under-guard.

They were telling him of twists and turns in the streets of the town, of crossing the square, of looking for a great colonnade, and doors leading to an arena. These doors were open, and watched by young men in red cloaks, with garlands in their hair. They would greet him, find him a straw pallet, and tell him what to do.

My indignation knew no bounds, hearing all this. For a moment I thought he could not possibly intend simply to desert us; it seemed to me such a mean and selfish act. But he thanked them; they opened the door for him, and he disappeared into the city.

Six

When the dawn broke we were huddled round our dead fire on a wide rocky strand below a cliff, and from end to end of the strand, lapped with silken water, iridescent in the morning light, no other person could be seen. 'It's no use looking for the Nikathlon,' I said. And I told them what I had seen last night.

'Why should we care?' said Niko, but we were all uneasy, as though some child we had been entrusted with had gone missing. 'We didn't ask for him,' he said, crossly. 'We didn't want him to come with us.' And that was true, of course.

'This is an island,' said Dio. 'And he hasn't got a boat. So doubtless we shall soon catch up with him. What we will do now is eat what we have, and go and search out these Games.' And Dio of course was in charge, the torch had put him in charge, burning steadily and quietly, with the low flame with which it met the morning. We did what Dio said. As soon as the path we were taking turned inland and joined other paths, we found ourselves in a crowd. The island tracks were thronged with people, all in bright clothing, and laughing and talking and bringing their children, as though for some festival. We would have been invisible among so many, we would have escaped attention entirely, but for the torch. It was rather hard to make the torch inconspicuous. It was burning with a bright blue, steady flame, and the morning sun blazed on the silver cone in Dio's hand, as bright as the flame itself. It looked strange; so much an Ago thing. Soon someone challenged us; a dignified man of forty

50

or so. He put a hand on Dio's arm, and pointing to the torch he asked, 'What's that? Why are you carrying that?'

Dio said, 'This is the torch from Olim. We are bringing it to your Games. It is a holy thing; a sign.'

'Well!' the man said. 'Our Archon is playing the dark horse indeed to spring such a thing on us. I am on the committee, and this is the first I have heard of it.'

'The Archon has not yet heard of it, either,' said Dio. 'We come of our own accord; nobody invited us, nobody ordered us to come. Shall we have a welcome, do you think?'

'Stand aside from the press of folk, and tell me more,' the man said. He drew Dio to one side, and I clambered up a boulder, and looked at the view. It was an island of rocks and flowers. Little streams tumbled between the rocks, and overgrown and neglected olive groves covered the ribbon of plain between the path we were on and the sea. Parties of islanders trooped past us, some of them singing, and carrying baskets of food for the day.

By and by Dio called us. He told us that we were under the protection of Yannis, who would take us straight to the committee for the Games. 'We are to follow Yannis's party, who are all wearing red. We shall tell them about the torch. Perhaps this is where the torch is supposed to be brought,' he said. 'Perhaps the job is done.' And he set off.

But Cassie, trotting along beside me, said, 'It isn't.'

That scared me. Cassie just knew things.

'Cassie, how do you know?' I asked her. 'You don't know that.'

She didn't answer.

'What does it feel like to know things you don't know?' I asked. 'When did it start?'

'It's been always,' she said. 'The day my brother went out to fetch the goats and fell to his death from a crag, I cried and wept, and hammered the sides of the pen they kept me safe in — for I was only a babe that day. My mother was

51

angry with me for the fuss I was making. But when the news came home she looked askance at me, and never loved me again. "She has a loathsome gift," my mother says, and she begs me never to fret or cry in the hearing of the neighbours, even if I saw the end of the world at hand.'

'And now?'

'Now. I know that these aren't the right Games.'

'But Cassie, *how?*'

'There's a sort of faint feel of danger somewhere.'

'From this Yannis?'

'From somewhere further.'

'But you can somehow see it?'

'That's the trouble with the gift. They call it second sight, but it isn't like sight at all. Nothing clear about it, nothing transparent. Just a murky lurching in the guts. I've felt afraid from the first moment we left the marble fields; I only came because of the torch. I'm very fond of you, Cal, of course, but . . .'

'But the torch has a good feel, Cassie?'

'Perhaps I mean a feel of goodness; but it's quite clear, as clear to me as morning light, as audible as birdsong, although dark and silent.'

She silenced me. She spoke so strangely, for a little girl.

We went, torch and all, where Yannis led us. He led us along paths that soon became highways, inland and downhill, to a city on a plain. A walled city, with armed gates. The gates, I thought, were larger and grander than the one I had seen last night; that must have been a postern, on a little-used approach. The crowds thronged through, and we went with them. They were going to a huge stadium, more than a mile long, which spread behind the city, seawards along a cliff top; or so it seemed, for the further end of the cursus seemed to touch the sky. At the nearer end were rows and rows of seats, rapidly filling with spectators, and a courtyard full of notices, bustle, changing-rooms. Yannis led us to an inner door, and took us through into sudden silence, to a council chamber, within which sat a dozen or so grey-haired old men in conference.

They wanted to speak with Dio, alone. In sudden alarm he turned to Peri, to stand beside him; and Cassie and Niko and I were turned loose, to our own devices. The feel of danger had crept a little closer, but it was not in the committee where we had left the two boys.

'I'll bet the Nikathlon is here, somewhere,' said Cassie. 'Do you want to look for him?'

'Yukk, no. But I'll bet he is.'

A great hum of excited voices directed our attention to the far end of the forecourt where a robed official was climbing on to a stand, and a press of people was gathering close around him.

'What's happening?' I asked a woman with a babe in her arms, who was standing near me.

'The announcement of the result of the heats,' she said. 'The list of those chosen for the great race.'

We walked across to the podium ourselves. The press of people was thick, and we couldn't wriggle through to the front. A drumbeat was sounded, and then the official began to call out names. He had a kind of tally-stick in his hands, which he fingered as he shouted out the lists. The people gradually dispersed as the names were announced, and we were able to get closer.

And then we heard 'The Nikathlon of Skiados, off-islander . . .'

'That's him!' said Cassie.

'Ran like the devil, that one,' said a young man standing near us. 'You'd think he wanted to win!'

'Oh, he does,' I said. 'He does. Will he, do you think?'

'Not likely,' said the young man. 'An off-islander isn't likely to win. There might be trouble. Might cause an international incident.'

'Do you mean the race is fixed?' said Niko, indignantly.

The young man looked uneasy at once. He glanced round, swiftly, and then said to us in a low voice, 'Look, there probably isn't any risk to it. Almost certainly. But . . . you are very obviously strangers here. You don't know much. And that friend of yours is amazingly good. He just might . . . If you get a chance, tell him not to try too hard, OK?'

'What do you mean?' I said. 'We don't understand . . .'

But the young man had melted away, simply stepping backwards and disappearing in the press of people. We looked at each other in dismay.

Cassie turned to a girl of about her own age who was passing, and asked her, 'Can you tell me, what's the prize in this race?'

'There's a cow and a calf for the second place, and amber beads for third . . .' she said.

'And the winner?'

'All honour to the winner,' she said, 'who honours the great god.' And coldness entered my mind. Fear.

'Cal, we had better try to tell the Nikathlon to go easy . . .' Cassie said.

I ran after the girl. 'Where are the runners now?' I asked her.

'In the training-halls,' she said. 'There's less than an hour before the race.'

'Could we get in? To see someone?'

She pulled a face. 'You could try saying you were bringing something. That he had forgotten his sweatband. That sort of thing.'

'We haven't got a sweatband,' I said.

'Here,' she said. 'I was taking one to my brother, and I picked up two by mistake. You could take this one and try to talk your way in.' She looked at me sharply, and, I thought, kindly. 'The winner will win, you know,' she said. 'And that's that . . .'

We sent Niko. He looked so small and waif-like, so incapable of harm that we thought he would get past, and so he did – simply waving the sweatband at the laughing young men who stood at the training-hall door, and slipping past them. Cassie and I stood a little way off and watched the crowds. We had never seen so many people before in our whole lives, not even on market days, and I was beginning to feel panicked by them – so many, so busy, so noisy, all with lives and purposes of their own, all milling about . . . their voices had a strangeness on them, and they wore their clothes in a fashion slightly different from ours, and this holiday they were keeping was nothing that we knew . . . I reached for Cassie's hand, and she did not shake me off. But that faint sounding note of danger still rang somewhere in the background of my mind, as though her gift had been catching.

'We shouldn't have let ourselves be parted like this,' I said. 'We should keep close together.'

'We should have,' she said, miserably.

'We might never find the others again in all this crowd,' I said. 'But I didn't think . . .'

'How could you have known?' she said. 'We've never been anywhere except the mountainside runs. We didn't have to keep together for dear life there . . .'

'I wish I was safe at home!' I said.

'Locked up with Dio's mother and never let out to play?' she said harshly, and she smiled at me suddenly. 'No. Well, perhaps you're right, after all we're running to meet trouble. Nothing awful has happened yet.'

Just then Niko reappeared, pulling a face at us.

'What did you tell him?' we asked.

'That it would be a good idea to come second.'

'And what did he say?'

'That I had the soul of a pig and didn't know anything about anything, and that he was the Nikathlon, bla bla bla!' said Niko, disgustedly.

'But what can we do?' I wailed.

55

'Nothing,' said Niko. 'You know, I see his point in a way.'

'*Do* you, Niko?' I said, amazed. 'Well, try telling us. Because I don't!'

'Well, he's just a freaker, isn't he? He only cares about winning. And we ask him not to try for the only thing he cares about, because some old woman in the crowd muttered at us. It's like asking Dio to dump the torch; or Peri not to trail around after Dio, or Cal . . .'

'Yes, OK, I get it,' I said, not eager to have the little beast get as far as me in his sharp-eyed list of freakouts.

'Oh, and he said to get a good view of his triumph we should go to the cliff-edge,' Niko added. 'They run this one the wrong way round; it begins and ends out there on the cliff, and the half-way post is back here in the arena.'

So we walked out along the running-track, with a long stream of other people going to choose viewpoints. It was a vast track, far longer than a normal person in normal health could have run without getting winded; and the race would be there and back.

The course was across a grassy level, cleared of stones and scythed of grasses and flowers, gently ascending from the stadium buildings behind us. All along it, on either side of a wide expanse of the course, people were lining up, settling on rocks and benches and on the ground. At the far end the ground dropped abruptly sheer into the sea, and we could glimpse a sandy shore and the blue waters of a bay formed by the headland we were walking on. At the very edge of the cliff a dais had been built, hung about with garlands of flowers, branches of olive and bay. In front of it was the starting line, a green ribbon stretched between poles. A half-circle of empty chairs awaited the arrival of the important people. There were tables to one side, with dozen upon dozen little silver bowls standing ready; there were officials bustling about, twitching things straight, smoothing wrinkles in the clothes on the table, glancing anxiously at the sky, though not a cloud was in sight, and a light breeze from the sea gently cooled a bright and blazing morning. Already every vantage point for yards and yards in front of the starting line was camped upon by early comers; already we would be hard pressed to find a spot from which to see anything.

The press of people and the buzz of hundred upon hundred of excited voices was making me dizzy.

Then suddenly we were rescued. A tall man wearing the red cloak of an official in the Games approached us. 'Are you not with Dio from Olim,' he asked us, 'bringing the torch? I have been told to look out for you.'

'We came with the Torch-bearer,' I said. 'We travel with him.'

'Come with me,' the man said. 'Seats of honour are set aside for you.'

And he led us to places near the centre of the semicircle, just below the dais.

'Thank you!' Niko piped up. Being so small he would have had the least chance of any of us of seeing anything from the third row back in the crowd.

'Young sir, it is the least we can do to honour those who bring honour to our Games,' said the man, solemnly.

'Does the torch belong here, then, do you think?' Niko asked Cassie as we settled ourselves.

And she said only, 'I don't know.'

Soon a slow procession with singing and a drumbeat wound towards us down the course, led by garlanded greybeards, and women wearing white. They took their places behind us on the dais and to right and left of us, and behind them came the runners, walking in lines of four to the slow beat of the music. The runners lined up on our left. Lastly came three alone: a great man covered with badges of office, and Yannis, and between them Dio, holding the torch. They mounted the platform, and the elder stood up and began to speak.

'Islanders!' he said. 'We know that our proceedings are holy. The ceremonies we conduct today and every year are in honour of the sea-god, at whose pleasure we eat, who sends the fishes teeming, who washes on our shores the weed without which our fields languish. But this year for the first time recognition has been brought to us from off-island. Those off-islanders who so often mock and deride our holy ceremonies, who even deny that any god is in the sea, have now repented and as a sign of their contrition have sent us this boy priest with a holy thing from Ago. A light with which to light the race; a blessing of fire. This year we will burn the ribbon through; and when it falls, then let every runner run his best! But first let each one drink the runners' wine.'

One after another the runners advanced, and were given a measure of wine in one of the little silver bowls. They held it high, lowered it to their lips, said 'Poseidon!' and drank it back in one gulp. The empty bowl was tossed into a basket standing by, and the runners moved into position behind the ribbon.

We watched for the Nikathlon, and by and by we saw him. He did exactly what the others had done; someone had told him, or he had carefully watched. You wouldn't have known he wasn't a native. And, indeed, among these people he didn't stand out as he had done in his own village, or amongst us. He was tall, but so were almost all these runners; he was lithe and light-footed, but so were all of them. His radiant health and strength still shone from his fine body, naked to the waist, but every one of these runners, to our unaccustomed eyes, looked like the marble gods from the broken halls at Olim.

When everyone had drunk their holy drink and stepped into line, Dio came forward. He went to the post nearest us, and put the torch, dimmed by the bright daylight, I thought, to the silken green ribbon stretched across the course.

Nothing happened. As he put the torch to the ribbon, the flame that had burned constantly ever since we dipped it in the broken bowl at Olim simply went out. The ribbon was not even scorched.

A sort of gasp went up from the crowd. Dio stood there, dumbstruck. He blew at the torch and tried again. The crowd muttered angrily. He swept his knife from his belt and slashed the ribbon through. Away the runners went in a drumming of footfalls, all bunched together and struggling for place.

Dio stepped back, and at once two burly officials were beside him. 'Get that thing lit again before you cause a riot!' one of them hissed at him. He beckoned frantically for us. We blew at the torch, fanned it with our hands. The mecho in the middle was blackened and sticky. Someone handed us a lighted candle, from somewhere near. We put the candle to the mecho, to the discoloured blue fuel, in vain. We were in a panic, all of us. It had never occurred to us that the torch might burn out so soon. And didn't I remember dimly, among all the other talk at Skiados, something about how the Ago torches couldn't be re-lit? Certainly we couldn't re-light this one, now. I felt us buffeted by waves of anger from everyone around us.

'Put the damn thing out of sight, and sit down!' the elder commanded us.

And when we did so we saw the runners returning, already half-way down the second lap, racing towards us. A red ribbon for a finishing line had replaced the green one. Most of the runners were still bunched, running close together. But out in front were two: the Nikathlon leading, with another boy at his right shoulder, only a step behind. Something made me glance at Cassie, and I saw that she was white-faced and trembling. Fear choked me. I knew that something evil, something terrible, was upon us . . . I didn't know what it was. And it was beautiful to see the Nikathlon run. He ran not only faster than all the world beside, but with such grace, such balance and rhythm. He made you see a runner's body as an engine designed to run, and designed for that only; while he moved you could think of a body as an Ago thing, a marvellous mecho, something done with craft no longer mastered by any living person . . .

Until the last minute we thought he was going to win. He was leading all the way. But in the last few metres the boy behind him suddenly overtook him. The boy behind him, twitching and lurching frantically, shot past him, fell across the ribbon, bearing it to the ground, stumbled sideways, and collapsed at our feet. The Nikathlon slowed down and stopped with an expression of stunned disbelief on his face.

But the winner was still moving. In spasm after spasm his back was ricked into a curve. He jerked, and rolled around. His face was blue, and a stinking green froth bubbled on his lips. We all saw it. The Nikathlon saw it.

'Foul play!' he cried. 'This man has cheated! He has taken a running drug . . . he should be disqualified!'

A burly official seized the Nikathlon bodily, clapping a hand over his mouth and bearing him away to a red tent pitched some way off. A rattling sound came from the throat of the winner. But no one helped him. They clapped him. They set a garland on his heaving chest. The drummer sounded up a slow beat, the singers began to intone a solemn song. Two red-robed young men picked up the winner, and held him high above their heads. He was still twitching, still arching his back.

'Oh great god of the sea, remember us!' cried the elder. 'Send the fishes to our nets all season long! For we give you the flower of the island, we give you the best we have!' And with that, leaping up on the dais, running to the back of it, to the very brink, the two young men carrying the winner cast him into the sea.

Seven

I wailed. I threw back my head and howled with shock, and
though Peri reproached me later, and said he thought we
might have slipped away unnoticed but for that, I think that
was unfair of him. We could not possibly have slipped away,
all of us, all in prominent positions, from so angry and so
pressing a crowd; and, after all, I had seen murder done.

Anyway, foolish or not, I did cry out. And the red-cloaked
officials swarmed around us, and hustled us roughly away,
towards the red tent where they had taken the Nikathlon.
There they held us prisoners, lined up against a wattle wall
at the back of the tent. Dio held the extinct torch close,
holding it to his chest as a child holds a harvest doll. He was
white-faced, frozen-faced, and the misery of his mind
drenched me as though it had been winter rain upon my
head. The Nikathlon was sitting crouched down with his
face turned away from us, no less miserable than Dio.

One by one the great men of the island, the wardens of
the Games, came in and sat down at a table, and scowled at
us. At last every seat was taken, and the great elder said,
quite softly, and speaking to his fellows, not to us, 'The
penalty for insulting or disrupting the Games is death.'

One of them said, 'They are ignorant, sottish strangers.
They did not know what they were doing.'

'Did we ask them to come here?' the elder said. 'Did we
want them? Did we put ourselves under any obligation to
explain ourselves to such as these?'

'They came at their own risk,' the second man agreed.

'Well then . . .' said the elder, shrugging.

'This business about the torch concerns me a little,' said a man from the end of the table. He was younger than most of them, and sat askew, studying us carefully. 'The fact is, I *have* heard of the wretched thing. My grandmother remembered something about it. And then, you see, there's no doubt it really is an Ago thing. One has only to look at it. And I had the impression the boy was genuinely trying to burn the ribbon, as he agreed to do. It strikes me perhaps he really didn't know it was about to go out.'

'But does that make any difference?' said the elder. 'Accidents happen.'

'Which threaten us. We tell everyone that a blessing is being conferred; when the damn thing goes out it looks more like a curse. And plenty of people were standing near enough to see what happened. It will be all round the island by now.'

'I agree,' said a man sitting near the elder. 'And we can only use the race for losing trouble-makers if the plebs think it is all quite straight and terribly holy. We have got to execute this little mob of visitors to keep up appearances. And before the last event when everyone goes home.'

'If we execute off-islanders,' said the one I now thought of as our defender, 'there may be repercussions.'

'Runaways, merely. Surely not,' said the elder.

'The trouble with that, brother, is that it is based on precedent. Every precedent we have suggests that nobody will come later asking about children, tinkers, minstrels, scruffy runaways. That nobody will make trouble over such as these. But we have no precedent for the torch. We have never had any such thing brought to us before. Perhaps somebody will be concerned about it . . .'

'I don't see the difficulty,' said a man from the far end of the table. 'We take care about the torch party. As you say, we have no precedent. We should give them the dry death by water. If anyone ever asks, we shall say that they came, and they left. But our own mob will be impressed by it, sufficiently. And we can also have an execution for immediate effect; we can flog and behead this stupid loudmouth who cried cheat.' He pointed at the Nikathlon. 'He has nothing to do with them.'

'Yes he has,' said Dio suddenly. 'He came with us. He is one of us.'

The Nikathlon looked up at Dio, startled.

At that moment an official suddenly appeared at the door of the tent, dragging a struggling urchin. He thrust his captive by the scruff of his garments up against a tent pole and tied him there, still fighting. Then he stood back; the urchin saw the assembled great men, let out a strange sound, like a cross between a whine and a grunt, and fell silent, and stayed still.

'What's this?' asked the elder.

'Taking bets on the javelin contest,' said the officer, throwing down on the table a handful of tinny coins. The elder, with an expression of extreme disgust, extended an index finger and spread the coins out to count them. 'A cheap life,' he remarked.

'A fair price, I should imagine,' offered another elder, glancing scornfully at the urchin who now had his eyes screwed tight shut as though to shut out the world.

'Come, come, then, what have we decided?' said the Prefect. 'The next race will be about to begin.'

'We should play safe,' said the elder who had defended us. 'Put the athlete in with the torch-bearers. But I see no reason against executing this trash . . .'

'Unless,' said the Prefect icily, addressing Dio, 'you lay claim to him too?'

'Certainly I do,' said Dio, coolly. 'He too came with us.'

'Laying bets on the sacred Games is just the sort of trick our native-born trash get up to,' remarked the elder.

'We have no money for food,' said Peri. 'We told him to.'

'Is this true?' asked the elder, addressing the raggedy boy.

'Yessir!' he said, croaking with fright.

'Is what true?' demanded the elder again.

'Everyfink what anyone says, sir!'

'Ludicrous,' said the elder. 'Quite ludicrous. But we are short of time.'

And indeed, as he spoke a flourish of trumpets sounded from outside, announcing another event. They left us, under guard.

'Does anyone know what the dry death by water *is*?' I asked.

'It sounds horrible,' said Niko.

'Well, it doesn't sound as bad as the other,' Cassie told him.

'You didn't have to admit I was with you,' said the Nikathlon, in a while.

'But you were with us,' Dio said, 'even if you didn't want to be.'

'What about me?' muttered the urchin. But we all fell silent. I was shaking slightly, as though I was freezing cold, though the tent was warm, full of sunlight filtered through the red cloth, and sheltered from the breeze.

We heard the crowd roaring and cheering for some other winner. Then the elders all came back, and guards seized us, and we were frog-marched out of the tent and down the length of the course, with staring eyes by the hundreds bent on us. Along the course, with people shouting curses at us, and ill-wishing us all the way. And down a sloping, stepped donkey-track to a little harbour, and down some weedy steps ... They put us all into a little cockle-shell boat, tied by its painter to one far bigger. They handed down to us the torch, and a clay water-pot stoppered with a chunk of cork. And then they towed us out to sea.

On and on they rowed us, in a deepening sunset, until the land, with dusk and distance, faded from sight. Then they rowed round in a ring, so that we no longer knew which way was which. Though knowing could hardly have helped us, in a boat with no oars, no rowlocks, no mast, no sail. We could see now all too well what the dry death by water was likely to mean. Then someone leaned over the stern of the towing boat, and with a blade that flashed ruby in the last rays of the sun, he cut the painter. They rowed away rapidly, leaving us adrift, in a calm approaching night, in a boat weighed down nearly to the gunwales so that it seemed ready to founder in the first wave that found us.

We sat in silence at first. Despair engulfed us. Or it engulfed me; Dio said sharply now and then, 'Sit still! Sit still; we mustn't capsize . . .' – as though he thought we had anything to lose; as though if we capsized we would be worse off. We were very cold; I could hear the urchin's teeth rattling together, until he put a thumb in his mouth to separate them, and began to moan softly, and rock himself, rhythmically banging his head on the gunwale. However still we sat, water slopped into the boat from time to time; we had no space in which to bail, and nothing to bail with except the jar containing our only water. Icy stars spread over the night above our heads like dew on the pastures of morning.

Then the Nikathlon said, 'Throw me overboard. I haven't the nerve to jump.'

'Don't be stupid,' said Dio.

'You'll have more freeboard,' the Nikathlon said. 'I don't care. I'd rather. If I stand up, someone push me.'

'Sit down, you'll have us all in the water!' said Dio.

My sharp and deepening dislike of the Nikathlon stung me. 'What is this?' I asked him. I couldn't see him; I talked in the direction of his voice in the dark. 'Just because you lost a race?'

'The winner was drugged,' he said, and added in a leaden whisper, 'I killed him, in a way.'

'Oh, don't!' I cried. 'Whatever can you mean!'

'There are lots of drugs you can take to make you go faster,' he said, wearily. 'But if you push yourself too hard with that in your bloodstream, you collapse and die. He must have thought to win quite easily, but I was there; I pushed him, I paced him too hard . . .'

'But he beat all the others anyway,' said Peri. 'And the winner was cast into the sea. If you hadn't pushed him hard, he still wouldn't have lived.'

'We all heard them talking,' Cassie said. 'They put the drug in those silver bowls. They did it deliberately, to get rid of people. The boy who won probably didn't know, didn't realize he was drugged.'

'I always thought of Games as the finest thing,' the Nikathlon said. 'The only thing people did that wasn't for gain. The fairest and the cleanest thing . . .'

'The ones we are taking the torch to are like that,' said Cassie, 'aren't they, Dio? The fairest and the cleanest contest in the world . . .'

'You're nuts, you are!' said the urchin, suddenly. 'We aren't going anywhere except getting drownded.'

'And the torch is out,' said Dio.

But not even the grief in Dio's voice could divert the Nikathlon. 'I wish I had died before I ran in a dirty race,' he said. 'When I stand up, push me.'

'What is your name, Nikathlon?' Cassie asked, suddenly.

'What does it matter?' he said.

66

'You ran as Nikathlon; your name was on the list as Nikathlon, wasn't it? And you didn't win; you aren't Nikathlon any more. When we find the true Games you can run as yourself. So what's your name?'

'My name is Philip,' he said, very softly. 'But why are you doing this? Why should you care about me?'

'You are with us,' said Dio, as though that settled it.

'But I . . . I wouldn't help make the fire.'

'It's not a question of what you are like, Philip the Nikathlon,' said Dio. 'It's because of what we are like. Stop feeling sorry for yourself, and sit still.'

We were quiet for a moment. I realized that I was no longer cold; that though my feet were up to the shins in water, something was warming me a little . . . *it was the torch!* I was sitting next to Dio, near the metal cone of the torch, and it was giving out heat. 'Dio! Can you feel . . .?' I asked him.

'I thought we could never re-light it . . .' he said.

'But perhaps it didn't go right out . . .'

And just then the torch sprang to life again. A bright flame leapt from the wick, and burned in a golden crown. It dimly lit our crouching forms, soaked, clammy, miserable; it showed us the depth of water in the boat, and the rising swell rocking us nearer and nearer to foundering. But it burned so brightly; and it warmed us as though it had been a great bonfire we were sitting round.

We reached out to it. We all laid hands on the chased and engraved metal from which it was made, and the warm light and brightening light it shed showed us each other's unguarded faces, with a ring of images of the fiery corolla of the torch dancing in the widened pupils of our eyes.

'I'm thirsty,' said Philip. 'Can we drink from that jar?' and we opened the jar, and found the water in it was heavily salted.

'Never mind, never mind!' I said, for somehow while the torch was blazing I could not feel despair. 'We can empty it and use it for bailing!' I took it, and began to work, leaning down to dip and fill it, and straightening up to pour it out over the side. Under my breath I began to sing as I worked.

And the torch burned brighter still. A huge flame roared up from it, so that Dio, in alarm, held it high out of harm's way. And as he did so we all heard the rhythmic beating sound of something across the water, and saw a wall of lights like a massive floating house. A huge ship was bearing down on us, but not to run us down. They shone beams of light on us across the water, and shouted and called.

We were not going to drown, nor die of thirst. We were going to be rescued.

Eight

We were blinded by searchlights. At first they cast a catnet over the side of their vessel, supposing we would be able to climb up. We were too weak for that. We tried, of course, and in trying we upset our swamped and foundering boat; it sank away under us, leaving me and Philip clinging to the lower edge of the net, and the others in the water. Dio sank in the boat and the torch went under with him, hissing as it vanished. I let out a wail of terror, and at once, with a rattling of chains, a lifeboat was lowered a yard or two across from the nets, and the seamen in it began hauling the swimmers out of the water. 'How many?' they were calling. I heard Cassie crying for Niko, and I thought we might have lost him after all. Then he answered from somewhere a little way off, and the searchlight above us swung away from the ship and lit him, holding on to the empty water-bottle, keeping himself precariously afloat. 'The urchin!' I called. 'What about him?'

'I've got him!' came Peri's voice, below me. Again the lights swung. Peri was treading water at the foot of the net, holding on with one hand, and holding the urchin by the scruff of the neck with the other. They simply pulled the net up again with us clinging to it, so that we were scooped over the rail and dumped on the deck like a haul of mullet with a debris of weed and shell. Dio held the quenched torch to his chest, and hung his head. I thought he might be crying over it, but we were all dripping and flowing with water anyway; I couldn't see tears. Then the blinding lights were switched off, and in the pitch darkness before our eyes adjusted a deep voice remarked in a strange accent, 'That's one hell of a warning flare you were showing! What the hell kind is that?'

'It's gone out,' said Dio. 'We've lost it.'

'Served its turn though,' said the voice. Gradually we could make out, by the treacly glow of ordinary decklights, that the voice came from a uniformed figure standing just beside the wheel. 'We saw you maybe three miles off. Doesn't owe you much.'

Dio shook his head, and didn't answer.

'Get them below and dry,' said the officer. 'The Company will have my head on a plate if we lose more time.'

By the time we were dry, had had hot showers, and put on shirts and overalls, far too big for us, while our homespun garments steamed gently on the hot pipes that ran through the cabin they gave us; by the time we had eaten platefuls of thick stew and coarse bread, and the ship's doctor had visited us and slapped ointment on the scrapes and grazes we had suffered while being dragged on board; by the time we had taken the tot of rum he prescribed against the cold, we were all asleep in our chairs, and barely able to stagger to the bunks they allotted us, roll into them and sleep.

We awoke in daytime, many miles from the point where they had picked us up, to find ourselves steaming along aboard a vast, rusty cargo ship, with a crew of thirteen men, the doctor, serving punishment time, we understood, for some nameless wickedness, and a cook. We took ourselves to the lower stern deck, where we could crouch on a mess of twisted hawser and a pile of tatty lifejackets and confer together, while the engines pounded and thumped and the wake streamed out behind us.

'What are we going to do?' Dio asked us. 'While the torch was burning I knew what we were doing. We were taking it to the Games.'

70

'And now?' I asked.

'Now I don't know. Without the torch we might as well go home. Or, at least, some of us might. I can't, and Cal can't; but the rest of you must feel free. Go home if you want.'

'Why can't you go wherever it is?' asked the urchin.

'I got Cal into trouble. If we went back things would be terrible for her, and it's my fault. So I'm looking after her somehow . . .'

I looked down. Of course, I was glad Dio was looking after me. But I said, 'You don't have to.'

'I think I do,' he said.

'Think it through, Dio,' said Peri. 'We can't really just go back. It's a long way, for one thing, and getting longer. And none of us would be sure of what welcome we would have.'

'So?' said Dio.

'We'd better stick together and see if we can find somewhere.'

'What about the urchin?' said Cassie. 'He might rather slip away.'

'Why do you think that?' I asked her. I had assumed the urchin would be desperately grateful to us.

'He thinks we're mad,' she said.

The urchin looked at her, startled. 'I never said!' he exclaimed.

'But you do,' she said flatly.

'Well, who wouldn't?' he said suddenly. 'Have I got you right, mate?' He turned to Dio. 'If this thing was still burning, you'd be happy to cart it around the world looking for something it was for?'

'Yes,' said Dio.

'Well, why?'

'Why what?' said Dio.

'Why would you do it?'

71

'It was laid on me,' said Dio. 'The Guardian asked it of me.'

'But you don't have to. You don't have to do what some old dead geezer said, do you?'

'I don't have to,' said Dio. 'But I would.'

'Well, you're nuts, you are!' the urchin said triumphantly. 'Course I'll go wif yer . . . Cor!' He broke off, wide-eyed. The torch, which was lying at Dio's feet, had begun hissing faintly. Dio picked it up. It steamed like a boiling kettle.

'Cor!' said the urchin, and reached out a grubby hand to touch the shining metal of the cone.

The torch stopped hissing, and put forth a little tongue of fire, burning low and steady like a candle in a windless room.

The Captain was friendly, but adamant. The ship couldn't change course for us, or call at an unknown and possibly hostile port. She was making passage to Benghazi, and he would take us there. Or to his next port of call, at Marsay, if we preferred. And while embarked with him we could work for our keep. Washing decks and coiling ropes and suchlike. Nothing too hard. What he really wanted was a chance for the ship's engineer to examine the torch. I didn't like the sound of that, but Dio said, 'Perhaps it would help if we understood it better.'

'It does act strange,' the urchin offered.

But the ship's engineer couldn't cast any light on the strangeness. Or not much. The round thing in the middle of the torch he called a burner. He said he could see it was designed to draw in air from the outside to regulate and ventilate the flame. It was self-adjusting, he said; perhaps that accounted for the sudden going out and re-lighting we told him about. But the real oddity to him, we gathered, was the fuel. He couldn't guess what it was, except that it wasn't anything he could get a supply of now, and use to make ship's lanterns, or maroons, or whatever the Captain had been hoping. He dug a little chunk of it out on the tip of his penknife, and considered it.

'The thing is, it's solid,' he said. 'I suppose it must liquefy somehow, to soak that wick and burn. If it was like candle wax the fire would soon burn down into the hollow of the cone and you wouldn't see it any more. Of course, if I could take the thing apart . . .'

'No,' said Dio.

'Well, of course not,' the engineer said. 'But if it goes out again you could try holding it upside down for a bit . . . and I wouldn't dunk it in salt water too often either, mate. Not every day of the week. Not many naked flames are waterproof.'

'We were told it could never be re-lit,' I said.

'Well, I can't see where it lights,' the engineer said. 'What did you do to light it in the first place?'

'It had a bit of cotton tape sticking out. Like a wick.'

'Well, that has obviously burnt down inside the mecho. You probably can't reach it any more.'

'Has it got a lot of fuel? How long will it burn?'

'Hard to say. That burner regulates how brightly it burns, and that must influence the rate at which it uses up its fuel. How long since you lit it?'

'A couple of weeks.'

'Well, it hasn't used much yet. It seems full. Unless it's using it from the bottom first . . . can't be doing that . . . fact is you can't tell with Ago things. I should guess it's tanked up for a good long time, but I can't guess how long. Sorry.'

'Isn't there anything else you can tell us?' said Dio.

''Fraid not. You see, some Ago things are mechanical; they have moving parts, like the engines on this ship. If you

73

fiddle about with them, and look at them long enough, and think hard, you understand them. Well, how they work, anyway, though not how they were made. They must have had incredibly strong and accurate tools to make the things they did. If you need a spare part for something these days it has to be cut and filed to size by hand – there aren't very many craftsmen who can do it, and then it usually wears and grinds, doesn't fit exactly, in short. I have seen a turbine with gear teeth made of wood; the miller said they wore out all the time, but he had a man who could make more, whereas the metal ones the Ago designer put in just couldn't be replaced . . . but you see, there are other Ago things, and your torch is one of them, which don't have moving parts. They often have wires, wound in rings and coils, and sometimes mazes.'

'Mazes?' asked Dio.

'Little mazes, incredibly tiny and faint, which you can just see on plastic plates. The mazes have things welded on at all sorts of intersections. And nothing moves. Nobody understands those things now. But there were millions of them in the Ago. They must have done something. If we took that mecho out of your torch and stripped it down, that's what we'd find, I expect. A little thing the size of my thumbnail covered with a maze drawn by fairy fingers, and no use to us at all.'

'You sound sad,' said Cassie suddenly, putting a hand into the engineer's.

He looked down at her, and smiled. 'If you're an engineer you're always fighting losing battles,' he said, 'with wear and tear. Everything has a breaking point; everything fails sooner or later. This ship, for example, makes a living for all of us while it lasts, and won't last for ever. It isn't good to be on the downward slope of knowledge; fighting a losing battle with knowing what to do . . . As you say, I can't help you.

74

The man who made your torch was an engineer. And I'm an engineer. But the world's gone sour.'

So we weren't much further forward. Except to Benghazi.

'We've been thinking about you,' the Captain said. He had us all sitting round the map table in his cabin, with most of his officers. 'We want to help you. You were looking for games; competitions of some kind, we gather?'

Dio nodded. 'Our torch belongs somewhere. Where there are Games.'

'The world used to be full of that kind of thing, in the Ago, no doubt,' the Captain said. 'Now everyone's too busy scratching a living. Only one of us has ever heard tell of games, apart from the ones you escaped from, and that's Zach here.' He waved a hand at his purser.

'The desert tribes hold games,' said Zach. 'Famous races. That the sort of thing you mean?'

Dio nodded.

'They gather from all over once a year for them, feasting goes on for days. We've all heard of them, us that live on the coast. Never seen them, just the buzz of rumour; but then there's no love lost. None of us could go near them without being murdered for spies.'

'From what we gather,' the Captain took over, 'the coastal people, Zach's people, are more or less at war with the desert tribes. Always getting raided and looted. Needing to fortify their farms, that sort of thing. There aren't any safe ways to reach the desert from the coastal towns. Now we are making into a coastal harbour, you understand, with cargo to unload. We'd put you down in the wrong place, and we'd maybe get into trouble ourselves. So if you want to reach the interior, we think it would be easier if we put you off at night on one of the beaches, and you could strike inland from there before any of the coastal people knew anything about you.'

'We might have a long wait for Games that are only once a year,' I said.

He just wants to get rid of us, I was thinking.

'They are at the autumn equinox,' said Zach. 'You've got a fortnight or so to find them. It should be enough if you don't get into trouble or run out of water.'

'We'll give you water-bottles. Supplies. We seem to have a tent from some cunning trader somewhere. There isn't a market for tents; I can't think how I fell for that one. But you're welcome to it. If that's what you want to do, naturally.'

He's desperate to get rid of us, I thought. If we stay it will be to a poisoned welcome. And for that reason or another, Dio said, 'Yes.'

That's how we found ourselves put down on an uninhabited shore, at a point where the coastal strip was narrowest and the desert almost in sight from the sea, going southwards into a dry land, chasing a rumour of Games.

Nine

At first we crossed a rocky, hilly place, with a dusty track winding through small hills, hills all rough and craggy with outcrops of red rock. A thorny scrub of low bushes grew there. Lizards basked in the shadeless heat. Huge black birds with ragged, dirty plumage lumbered overhead. Peri was carrying the tent rolled up on his back, and each of the rest of us carried water. In someone's pack there was food. The Captain had given us all he could. We came from a hot country, from a place of burning light, but the heat soon defeated us. The torch itself seemed to shrink from the blazing sun, and burned with a low, blue, near invisible flame. The effort of walking did not make us perspire; instead our skins became foul and sticky, creeping and itching with the deposit of sweat that vanished instantly into the dry and ravenous air.

Niko kept falling behind. The urchin began making a dry whining sound between his teeth. Soon Dio said, 'We must stop. We must find shade, and wait for nightfall.'

'Shade?' said Peri, looking around. The thorn bushes cast a thin and fretted shadow for inches only, and all within the ambit of their long and nasty spines.

'There is a cave,' said Cassie. 'I think there is a cave, a little way ahead.'

'How do you know, clever-clever?' said Philip. 'Do you come here often?'

'We'll go and see,' said Dio, quietly. 'You, Philip. You go ahead a quarter of a mile or so and see. If you find shade, call us.'

We stood panting, blinking into the blinding glare. Philip disappeared into it over a little height, and almost at once we heard him calling. Just down the slope beyond the hillock there were two huge slabs of the red desert rock, tilted up, one leaning against the other. Between them was not a cave exactly, but a gap, in deep shade.

'You have eagle eyes,' said Philip. 'It was clever of you to spot this . . .' But Dio was looking at Cassie thoughtfully. Gratefully we scrambled in under the rocks, and lay down to rest in the soft sand sifted there. Then by moonlight we marched on. The thorn bushes spaced themselves out, grew fewer, shorter, vanished. And the land swept upwards and downwards in great heaving slopes like waves, became a sea of sand in which our shoes sank deeply at each tread. The night was cold, with a bitter clarity of stars and a biting presence that made us wrap ourselves in our cloaks. Our feet, however, sank through a skin of coolness on the face of the dunes into hot sand below the surface, that held the warmth of the day.

We lost all sense of time, going like that. Each day sleeping, usually in our tent for shade, sometimes under rocks. Each night marching in an unfailing moonlight, each dawn eating, making a camp . . . the food they had given us on the ship was a strange stuff in squares, dark brown, pungently sweet, and hard to chew. Whatever it was, it was good for us, and we felt no hunger. The water was much more difficult; we had no idea how long it would last, but a day came when I noticed we had now drunk more than half of it. We had not enough to go back; of how far on we would need to go, we had no knowledge. The desert dunes grew deeper and softer every day. We walked ever more slowly, as each step sank in and had to be dragged out of the clinging and sliding encumbering sand. I wondered if the others blamed Dio for their deaths; I was sure we each saw our own death just over the next swelling of the endless vistas of sand.

And I began to think, of course, to wonder about Dio. I lay in the blazing heat and light of the tent while we rested. The tent walls were rolled up an inch or two to give us any air that might be moving, though we seemed to choke anyway. The thin canvas barely seemed to break the violence of the light, and even with eyelids closed we flinched away from the brightness, and covered our sticky faces with our heavy arms. I slept only lightly, if at all, and dreamed shallow dreams that were barely distinct from memories. Dio as a little boy, naked, helping to drive the sheep into the stream to wash the wool, and running in and out of the water himself . . . my father would not let me cool myself by running in the shallows with Dio – could I have been hot, in Hellada? Memory recorded it as cool, pale, watery fresh air blowing under the olive trees, turning the leaves to show silver, between the fields of red earth, gashed by redder poppies . . . and always a sound of water running. Never more than a mile from water . . . when we grumbled and cursed fate in Hellada we didn't know our luck . . . But the day they wouldn't let me paddle with Dio he dipped his tabard in the water and brought it dripping wet, and wrapped it round me so that the soaking coolness reached my skin at once through the thin cotton I was wearing, and we both laughed. Around us, above us, I think – I must have been still the height of a small child – there was talk of farms . . . perhaps that was the day that led me to die in this terrible heat and dryness. The day of the tabard-dipping they had remembered that Dio and I were of an age, and had noticed that his family's land and my father's land abutted . . . On that day they had decided to give me to the mad boy for his own.

For surely Dio was mad? What were we doing, marching

into a fiery wilderness, bringing fire? Had the Guardian meant us to do any of this? What exactly had he said to Dio? Well, I hadn't heard every word, of course, but whatever he had said . . . While I was thinking these disloyal thoughts my face began to sting. A light breeze was moving on the surface of the sand, and tiny sharp grains were flicking against my skin. I sat up, and went out of the tent. The ground was smoking, it seemed, with a flurry of sand; the air above was still bright and clear. I untied the strings which held the tent off the ground, and trod the bottom edge of the canvas into the dune to make it sandproof. My ankles were stinging, scoured by the steady blast of sand. All round me the surface of the desert was damasked with running ribbons of sand, racing like winding torrents, weaving a fluid pattern inches above the ground. Then suddenly with a sound like gigantic gasping a tall wind rushed over the nearest dune crest and engulfed the world with flying sand. I could see nothing. My eyes were scratched and screwed tight shut with the pain. I staggered about and fell. Then I felt someone's hand on my ankle and, above the susurrating uproar of the storm in my ears, I heard Dio's voice calling my name. I crawled in the direction in which he was tugging, and he pulled me into the shelter of the tent.

It was hours before I could open my smarting eyes, and when I did the storm was still blowing. The tent had become silted up with sand. The finest grains were penetrating the canvas; the tent was full of choking, dusty air. Behind the canvas a load of sand weighed heavily on the tent walls. We were half buried. Peri and Dio kept bracing their backs against a section of the tent, and pushing till the sand ran off. They seemed to be fighting a losing battle. Our teeth grated on sand; sand itched in our nostrils and ears, and ran out of our hair when we moved. Niko brought me a sip of water, and whispered, 'I'm scared, Cal . . .'

So was I. Sparse tears ran out of my scratched eyes. I licked dry lips, and got sand on my tongue.

And then, as abruptly as it had come, the wind dropped. We could hear in the sudden, total silence the tiny sounds of the flying grains falling out of the air, the silken sounds of the drifts sliding off the tent, the new configurations of dunes arranging themselves, coming to rest in temporary stability.

Peri lifted the tent flap, kicking it free of the boulder with which we had weighted it to keep it shut, and we crawled out. I could not think what time of day it was; I blinked in the brightness, but it was not the terrible clear brightness of the days before. A dust like the mist of autumn hung everywhere; the light was clouded, grey. There were no shadows. There was no distance visible. We looked down, and Cassie cried out, shuddering. We saw bones. At our feet a pit had opened, so that our tent, which had been in a valley when we pitched it, stood now on the crest, the brink of a descent. And at the foot of the descent a dreadful confusion of skulls and bones projected from the sand. Wind-sculptured hollows and ridges, miniature dunes on the leeward side of each dry jutting knuckle and curved rib, exaggerated the pattern they made. Some of the skulls lay quiet like sleeping turtles, some stared at us, all were dry as sand, coloured like sand. We couldn't have counted. There were many.

Someone let out a whimper; I did, I think. Then we looked up; and there were shadows. Faint and far off, and moving. Shadows of rust and of indigo, pale colours through the dust. Shadows of riders, though in the blurred occlusion of the drifting sand their mounts looked gross, deformed; the riders' heads looked gross, gigantic. They were moving across the distance. And vanishing over a col of sandhill in a long line, almost single file, behind the riders, were walkers leading lumpen beasts. A human voice reached us – a single, bird-like cry.

We were afraid. I think we might have simply stood there and let them pass us by if they had not seen us. But suddenly, before we had found our tongues to utter a word to each other, to ask each other what to do, there was a rider towering above us, scarcely three paces away. We had not seen him leave the caravan and come. He loomed in a whirlwind of stirred sand which fell slowly away, revealing him clearly little by little, and the head first.

A head swathed in a huge turban of white cotton, covering him entirely except for a narrow slit for his eyes. Blue eyes stared through at us. A robe of blazing deep blue, faded intricately into every shade of sky or water, or midnight, or cornflower. His feet in the stirrups were clad in yellow pointed slippers. His pale and creamy steed was harnessed with a silver-mounted bridle on its fantastic head – a head that floated on an elongated neck, some way below a huge hump, covered with a carpet on which the rider perched. Long and knock-kneed legs with large splayed hooves supported it. And yet this monstrous thing had come like the wind, and arrived before we saw it moving . . . Behind the rider were two others, also in burning blue, emerging from the dust storm they themselves had raised, and these two, bafflingly, were crouched low in their saddles, their arms wrapped round their heads, whimpering slightly, and gazing at us askance with every appearance of terror.

The leading rider pointed to himself, and then swept a robed arm across the horizon, where the procession of shadows was still winding, and said, 'Twaag.' Then he pointed at us, and spread his hands.

'Greeks,' said Dio. 'Hellenes.'

The two attendants let out strangled moans.

'Have you any water?' asked Dio.

82

'Shutmouth!' said the leader, turning to his companions. 'Dead don't drink!' and he made a clicking sound, whereupon his beast lurched forwards, and folded its legs, bringing him within easy dismounting distance of the ground. He reached into the folds of baggage hanging from his saddle, and brought out a leather bottle, which he unstoppered and offered to Dio.

'Can we all have some?' Cassie asked.

'Yes. More not far,' the Twaag said.

'What's the matter with them?' asked Niko, licking his lips from his drink and pointing to the other two, who were still hanging back and staring at us.

The Twaag smiled, a smile hidden under the drape across his face, but showing in the bronzed wrinkles round his eyes. 'You stand up in the place of skulls,' he said, grinning, 'and call yourselves "Geeks", a name we give to spirits . . .'

'Greeks. We said Greeks,' said Dio.

'Allah, Allah!' said the third rider softly.

'He thinks you say "Geeks",' said the Twaag.

'Tell him it's all right,' said Niko.

'Not mind him,' said the Twaag, contemptuously. 'You come now. Here not good place.'

'We must dig out our tent, find our things,' said Dio. But the tent was lying almost flat under the drifts, and nothing could be seen anywhere of the bundles we had been carrying.

'Leave things,' the Twaag said. 'Not bring things from bad place. We give you better things. O K?'

'Only this,' said Dio. He brought the torch out suddenly from the fold of his cloak in which he had been holding it, and held it up. It flared crimson for a moment, and then died back to the small blue flame with which it had burned since we brought it to the desert. The Twaag leader looked at it in alarm.

'Not need that,' he said. 'The sun is enough, and more.'
'Not for us,' said Dio. 'This is a spirit light, and we are taking it to the Games.'

'Games are for nomad tribes only,' the man said. His voice had lost the steady boastful note of a few minutes ago. 'Secret. Only for blue people. You best not know.'

'We do know,' said Dio. 'Take us there.'

It was not, in fact, very far. Perhaps three hours' walk. But they made no haste. Just over the next rise of dunes they stopped for water. We would not have known there was any there; but they pointed out to us a different scrubby plant growing, and a sort of crusty cohesion of the shifting sands. They dug a little, and then the sand suddenly darkened, came out of the pit sticky and brown, and then clear water filled the hole. They dipped and filled their jars and bottles, and we filled ours too. Everybody drank, and by now it was dusk, and the rapid nightfall of the desert was upon us. They didn't make camp, pitch tent, or cook food. They just rolled themselves into blankets and lay down. Someone lent us a carpet, which we spread out, We lay under our cloaks, huddled together, and unsleeping, restless, under the bright stars. After all, we were not tired; we had not been marching, but sitting out the sandstorm. In the middle of the night – I don't know when, I can't tell time from the stars as Dio and Peri can – I got up and wandered off, stretching my cramped legs. There were a myriad small sounds in the stillness, the shifting of the recumbent camels, the tinkling of the metal on their bridles, a murmur of voices from one or other of the shadowy groups of sleeping forms. Only the faint blue spark of the torch led me back again, where Dio had thrust it into the sand upright beside his head.

And in the morning we could see others, moving. Lines of others on the horizon, or threading their way diagonally down a distant slope, others in every direction we looked, but all moving the same way, the same way as we. By noon we had reached our destination: a city engulfed in sand.

The first sight we had of it was the broken walls, jutting through the smoothness of the desert, desert-coloured, made of the desert mud, clearly man-made. The wind of many years had scoured and piled the sands, and half buried, half cleared it. A massive gateway still crossed the roadway in, and there were guards there, though in holiday mood, greeting arriving folk by name, laughing and gossiping. And now its dry and dune-filled streets were full of life. Seething throngs of people were arriving and digging in. Across the roofless houses the women were stretching awnings of bright canvas, saffron, purple and rust, simply laid over bundles of canes; children were sweeping and raking the sand to clear doorways, to make level places for the outspread carpets on which they sat and slept. Stalled in the next rooms their camels snorted and stamped. A wide street we came through was already starting as a market, with food and leatherwork, wrinkled dried fruits and nuts, silver clasps and woven dhurries spread out for sale or trade.

The Twaag led us confidently through the streets to a quarter of houses in somewhat better repair. By long tradition, he told us, each tribe had its own street, or patch of streets. I thought we might learn to tell the tribes apart, given time, for they seemed to like different colours, different patterns of sequins and beads, and only the Twaag kept their faces covered up to the bridge of the nose; the others showed dark, sun-browned faces, with wide mouths, and noses hooked like eagles. The Twaag would billet us amongst themselves, he told us, but we would have to appear before the King to get permission to stay. He gave us a good lodging, though; a room with the rafters still in place, though bare, which was easily made weatherproof with a stretch of canvas.

85

It gave on to a courtyard where the women were already setting up a hearth for cooking, and in which the men, digging vigorously through a sandhill that had blown into a corner, were busily uncovering a well.

They brought us gifts: the bale of canvas for our roof, rugs for the floor, a copper cooking-pot, a woven blanket, a draught of astonishingly cool water, a share of the supper. When we had eaten and were sitting quietly, the Twaag came to see us. 'You must stay here,' he said. 'Not let others see you tonight. Strangers not allowed at sacred festival; not allowed to know about races. Above all, not allowed to come. So I must tell King you are here, tell him where we found you, and of the spirit lamp. If he likes, he keeps you here, honoured guest. If not . . .'

'If not, what?' I murmured, but he took no notice.

'So tomorrow I take you. Soonest safest. But seeing King not easy. First we see advizier. He very difficult man, very dangerous. You shutup and leave talk to me. OK?'

'Why should we trust you to speak for us?' Dio asked. 'Are you our friend?'

'He who brings honoured guest is honoured host,' said the Twaag. 'Very good for my tribe, make other tribes very sick! We hope King likes you.'

'Let's all hope so,' said Dio. 'All right, we'll leave the tricky advizier to you.'

'Allah bring you sleep,' the Twaag said, retreating, and lowering the draped canvas door as he went.

The advizier was a huge man, tall and fat and sullen. He sat in a side room, off the entrance halls of the King, beside a broken marble basin that had once held a fountain, and now was half full of sand. He was eating as he received us, though he did not offer food, nor ask us to sit. We hung back, nervously. Cassie held my hand, and Niko held hers.

86

The Twaag was speaking, urgently, respectfully. He did not use English. We waited. Standing impassively behind the advizier's pile of cushions stood a bodyguard, waiting too. Seven of them, and all with little curved knives in their belts.

Dio stood furthest forward, holding the torch. Perhaps he thought the torch would be our ambassador. After all, it did impress people. But not here. Suddenly the Twaag's voice was raised in protest; he was talking swiftly, pleading. The advizier silenced him with a wave of the hand.

'This is what the King decides,' he said to us in English. 'The strange children will be put ten miles on the road north, and left there. One water-bottle will be given them. The torch they carry is forfeit; confiscated as a punishment for impudence. For the temerity of coming here, my dears,' he added, smiling at us.

'No,' said Dio.

'No?' said the advizier, laughing. 'How will you stop us?'

He spoke shortly to his bodyguard, who all sprang forward at once and surrounded Dio. Dio fought, but only for seconds. Then he was on the floor, and one of the bodyguard had a foot on his neck, pinning him down. It's hard to fight holding on to something. But the man who had wrested the torch out of Dio's hand held it aloft for less than a second, before dropping it, howling with pain. The whole shining metal body of the torch was glowing, as though it had become red hot.

It lay dully bright on the sand of the floor. The man who was holding Dio let him get up, and pushed him roughly back towards us. A babble of voices in English and other tongues surged round us. Dio made a dive as if to pick up the torch, and was pushed back. The advizier turned to the Twaag.

'You. Pick that up and bring it here,' he said.

87

The Twaag had gone pale. He pulled a fold of his cloak free, and wrapped it thickly round his right hand. He reached for the torch with muffled grasp, and twice dropped it. But it was only when he succeeded, and was carrying it towards the advizier's couch that the flame of the torch went out. It hissed, and died in a thick and stinking belch of black smoke.

Dio cried out in dismay. The advizier said, 'Idiot! Fool!' at the Twaag. And a quiet voice behind us said, 'What is happening here?', whereupon everyone but us hit the floor, bowing themselves down to the ground. Even the advizier.

'Who are you?' said Dio. He was still rubbing the side of his neck, and there was pain in his voice. 'Can you help us?'

'Perhaps,' said the newcomer. 'I am the King.'

Ten

I sat watching Dio, and Dio sat silent, the expired torch lying across his knees and his head in his hands, where he had been sitting all day. We were in a light and airy room, shaded by awnings from the sun, overlooking the stadium. The King's palace was built on the wall of the city, on the far side from the gate by which we had come in, overlooking the miles of sand-softened terraces, and the hard, flat, wind-swept floor of the place of the Games. A silver tray on intricate carved legs of its own stood beside Dio, laden with figs and apricots and nuts and little gilded leaves, and a jug of sherbet – not a morsel, not a drop of which he had touched. The King had helped us; the King had listened, the King had rewarded the Twaag, rebuked his advizier – 'But I cannot do without him,' he had told us. 'He is very clever. But clever people are sometimes stupid about holy things, don't you find?'

We could not re-light the torch. When first attempts failed, the King had suggested clean fire – and his imam had kindled it, struck from steel and stone, and lighting a taper that had been blessed three times. It would not rekindle the torch. Then the King had suggested that the torch was insulted, and made the advizier offer elaborate apologies to it, involving bowing and wailing. The torch took no notice. We all remembered being told that, once lit, it could not be re-lit; it had to burn with the very fire that sprang to life at Olim, or nothing. Even so, when we had told the King more he brought a silver bowl from his treasures, and we tried in the blazing desert noon to re-light the torch in that, holding it to the sun as we had the mirrored bowl, so many days ago. And that too had failed.

So now we were the King's guests, waited on by his servants, comfortable, and safe, and unhappy.

'Dio, do eat something,' I said. He shook his head.

'You are taking this too hard, friend,' said Peri. 'It might be all right, in a while.'

'It has happened before, after all,' I said. 'It seemed to go out, and then it hadn't.'

'Never for so long,' he said, dully. 'Never so cold.'

'But it *might* recover, Dio,' I insisted. 'We don't understand it. We don't know what it might do; we only know it's special.'

'I am afraid it isn't,' said Dio, bitterly. 'Don't you see what I am afraid of? Is it special, or is it quite ordinary, just something the Ago made for some job or other, not intended for us at all? Perhaps it's just run out of fuel. Just an ordinary lamp that has burnt all its fuel. What then?'

'Well then, we'd have been wasting our time,' I said, 'carrying it about the place. But we would get over it, I suppose.'

'But I don't see how we could get over it,' he said, his voice still very dull and quiet. 'From the first moment we encountered it, from the first moment we found the Guardian, it began to cost us dear. It began to uproot us, to make us do things which lost us our places at home. Not just mine, Cal, not just yours, but these others who have followed it with us. We have all displaced ourselves from where we belonged.'

'But it isn't your fault . . .'

'It is my doing. While it burned I knew what I was doing. I knew it was special, and we were serving it. Now it has gone out I am afraid that it is not special; that we are just

90

stupid. How can I lead you anywhere without the torch to carry?'

'You can lead as long as any of us follow,' said Cassie.

I stared at her. She had changed from being a delicate little girl to looking starved, anxious. Had she grown taller? Her eyes were full of a troubled expression. So that I wondered, not for the first time, but with a pang of anxiety, what she saw that I did not, what she knew that the rest of us didn't. I was becoming a little afraid of her, and also, when I saw the stamp of thinking on her face, afraid for her, for I loved her dearly. Now she said, looking coolly at Dio, 'You think you are wretched because the torch has gone out. But perhaps the torch has gone out because you are wretched.'

'You take it, then,' he said, turning on her. 'You take it and cheer it up! Get it away from me, and see!' And he put it down and kicked it, so that it rolled towards us on the marble floor. The taper of the stem made it roll in a wide section of a circle, slowly.

'No,' said Cassie as it rolled towards us. 'I can't. I really can't. You, Cal. You take it and I will come with you.'

So I picked it up as it rolled; it would have rolled on and back to Dio had I not. I picked it up and I was surprised at the weight of it. Somehow I had thought that it would be light, as if hollow, now that the fuel had run out . . .

'We are all going to see the competitions,' Peri said. 'Are you sure you won't come?'

Dio shook his head. We left him sitting, and we went out.

A vast assembly of people had gathered in the stadium below the King's palace. We wandered around, looking. Little platforms had been built along the length of the stadium, and round each one an expectant crowd was gathering. Luckily we met the Twaag almost at once. 'My friends,' he called. 'Come, come with me. I show you all the competition. I explain all. Later you tell the King how good I am . . .'

'This can't be a race,' said Philip, looking round. 'What sort of event is it?'

'The first day we compete for story-telling. Each tribe puts its best story forward. Second and third day, races. Then we must disperse.'

'Why do you come so far to such a ruined place anyway?' I asked him.

'Long ago this was the capital city of all the desert tribes, of all the blue peoples,' he said. 'The King ruled in splendour. Then the river ran dry, and the wells were sluggish. Now there is water for only three days in the year. We can dwell in our own city only for so long . . .'

'What made the wells dry up?' asked Peri.

'If I knew that . . .' said the Twaag expressively. 'Come, I show you the story-tellers . . .'

He told us at each booth the name of the tribe, the name of the famous teller who would try to win the crown, the number of people in the tribe, and the name of their patch of desert. Some he praised for silversmithing, some for carpet-making, some as desert guides . . . all this I forgot almost as soon as it was told me. One tribe he called Hassides, and blamed them for cruelty. The taking and trading of slaves was their special craft, he said. And right at the far end of the stadium we came upon an old man, sitting in a story-teller's booth, with nobody round him. The rush mats for his people were spread out ready, and not a single soul had chosen to sit down.

'Is this man very bad at it?' asked Philip.

'Good – bad, nobody know, makes no difference,' said the Twaag. 'This man very sad. His people all die out. He the last man left who speaks his language . . . he know it all by heart, all the history of his tribe from the first time they came to the desert . . . and no one left to understand him.'

'How can they judge his story?' asked Cassie.

'Not try. King send judges to listen to all the other story-tellers. No judges for him.'

'And he doesn't mind?' I asked.

'Perhaps he not know. He been blind many years. Nobody tell him judges not listening. You come now and sit with Twaag . . .'

'No,' said Cassie. 'Thank you, but we will sit here.'

The Twaag laughed. 'You not understand anything. He not tell in English like all the others. Go on very very long time!'

But Cassie had already sat down, cross-legged, on the matting. I planted the torch upright in the sand, and sat down beside her. A great gong sounded, and a hush fell in the stadium. The old man began to intone, uttering strange sounds, and rocking himself gently as he spoke.

He spoke at first very low, an inaudible mutter, as though speaking to the deaf; and we clapped softly, and called to him, and saw his blank face turn to us with an expression of amazement, and heard his voice lift and ring out strongly in a rhythmical, joyful flow.

And the strange thing was that we did in a way understand. In the long incantation we heard the sound of battles, the length of journeys, we heard the pain and despair, and sudden upsurges of triumph and joy. I heard the aching voice longing for times past, and it put into my mind the flowing waters of the river below the marble fields, the little white villages and red fields of home, and my mother's voice, crossed with love and complaint, droning on at me when the goats needed milking and water fetching and meal grinding, and I had been running among the poppies, and being a naughty child . . . In a while the urchin nestled up to me and put his thumb in his mouth, so that I thought he was falling asleep, but when I looked down at him I saw his eyes wide open. Cassie sat hugging her knees, her dark hair

93

screening her face from view, and beyond her Peri lay
sprawled, his head propped on one hand, but he too was
wide awake. Even Philip, who couldn't sit still for long
anywhere, paced up and down close by us and kept his eyes
on the story-teller. I wanted Dio to be with us. I missed him.

The voice went on and on. We heard the distant applause
as the other stories finished. The sun descended, and a
honey-coloured light glowed over us. Then as the sand of
the desert glowed rose pink, rose red, and the sky deepened
from lilac to indigo, and we began to see the stars faint but
strengthening above us, we realized we were no longer
alone. Now that all the other performances had finished,
curiosity had brought others to join us. A wide crowd had
settled down quietly behind us, so that as the story-teller
recounted how his people had died out one by one – or so I
guessed from the sound – his hearers one by one increased.
At last the King came too, and with him the crowd of
judges. Then in the dusk there was a perfume. A heavy and
delectable scent, like overblown roses, like the balsam pines
of the mountains. It was all around us, so that at first I did
not realize it was coming from the torch. But the King and
all his people saw what happened. As the long story finished
the torch leapt into life. No one was touching it; alone it
fired up, with a rainbow of coloured flame and a fragrance
like incense.

Cassie turned on me, in the lovely glow, a face full of joy.
The King advanced, and set a victor's crown of woven red
and silver on the old man's head, and the tribes whooped
and called and clapped . . . and I picked up the torch and
ran. I ran and ran, right down the stadium and up the
marble stairs, slipping and stumbling in my eagerness on
the sand-slicks that lay on every surface, and bursting into
the upper room I set the torch back in Dio's hands.

*

94

There was a feast that evening. The torch stood in glory on a low table laden with fruit and sweetmeats, and all around the room the King's guests – including the Twaag, overwhelmed with pleasure at being there – sat on carpets cross-legged, and drank and talked. A strange entertainment was laid on for the pleasure of the guests – a dance in which all the dancers were women, and all danced on their knees. They swayed, and moved their arms, and clicked their fingers, all to a rapid and accelerating drumbeat, and now and then one of them put her two hands to her mouth and uttered an extraordinary whooping cry, like the voice of some savage bird, or some unimaginable flute. The dance built up to a pitch of excitement, so that some of the men among the guests got up and joined in, thrumming their heels on the floor and spinning on the spot . . . 'Why are they kneeling all the time?' I asked the Twaag. 'This is a desert dance,' he said. 'You must imagine them dancing under the canvas of a low-pitched tent, while the sand-storm rages outside . . .'

I ought to have been enjoying myself. The food was good, and it was good also to feel important, to feel the protection of the King, to feel like a welcome person, not a suspect stranger. But I had eyes only for Dio, and took very little notice of anything else. Dio sat entranced, his eyes fixed on the steady burning of his torch. It seemed to cast in his direction its brightest, rosiest glow, and falling on his face it seemed to fire an answering, inner light. I was glad and cut to the heart by it at the same time. The expression on Dio's face was love. I had never seen such an expression directed at me. But then we had been forced on one another. It was not that which wounded me. It was more like fear. I had known that the torch needed us; it needed a Guardian, it needed to be carried, seeking its fortune. I had not understood that we needed it; that without it Dio would be lost . . .

Relying on Dio was one thing. I knew about him. He was young, and there were no obscurities in him. He was only a boy, and could only be leaned on like a boy; but I was not afraid to need him. But needing the torch was another thing altogether. We couldn't understand it; we couldn't predict it. Whatever it sought, wherever it wanted to be taken, it wasn't our safety or our good it was made for. I didn't like being beholden for life and death to something so fickle, something that could so easily be taken from us . . . I didn't like seeing on Dio's face a rapture that ought only to have been for a person, never for a thing, a mecho, an object . . .

Lost in thought, I missed the drift of all the excited talking. I came to myself to hear the King saying, 'Certainly there can be a tribe of the torch. Who is its eldest son?'

The Twaag showed a sudden twitch of alarm, and jumped to his feet. 'Sire, in the long conversations we have had, the torch-bearers and I, on the journeys which we took together after we rescued them in the drylands, I have discovered much about them . . .'

Philip snorted indignantly, and Cassie put out a hand to grip his wrist, and shot warning glances at him.

'. . . and I discovered the glorious descent of each and every one of them,' the Twaag was saying. The urchin preened himself, grinning, and helped himself to another handful of dates. 'The fact is, they are all eldest sons,' the Twaag said. 'Except, of course, those who are youngest daughters. Any of them may take part in tomorrow's race, with your blessing, sire. It is the race of the third day from which they are all debarred.'

The King bent on the Twaag a thoughtful expression, with, I thought, an element of surprise in it. It was obvious that the Twaag had used us to advance himself, and that the King didn't know him of old, as he did some of the other chieftains.

'My servant advises me well,' the King said in a moment nodding. 'I have heard him.' But I hadn't; I mean I hadn't heard the Twaag give the King advice, only tell him fibs about what he knew about us . . . The King turned to Dio. 'So any of you may run in the race of the eldest sons, tomorrow. But you will want to enter only the one who may bring honour to your tribe. Which of you runs fastest?'

'I do,' said Philip, at once.

But the King took no notice of him. He waited for Dio to answer.

'Peri will run for us,' said Dio. And as Philip jumped up, he added, 'and Philip. Philip is the Nikathlon,' he said, to the King. 'A title of honour in his own country, a title for victors.'

'Ah,' said the King, 'then we will honour him. Those whom we honour start further back,' he added.

Furiously scowling, Philip muttered, 'Not fair!' but Dio stared him into silence.

There has been nothing in our travels, nothing we have seen anywhere, like the race of the eldest sons. It seemed to me maybe it held into our tarnished and decaying times some of the glory of Ago, though the King said that in the stories of his peoples the racing came from before Ago: from unimaginably long past times. Glorious it certainly was. That huge arena, all decked with flags, and loud with drums and trumpets, and humming with a vast crowd! Busy though the ruined city had been, I had not realized how many people were gathered there till I saw the whole crowd. I had not known so many people were in the entire world, let alone that all of them had clothes of silver, clothes of scarlet, ribbons and jewels to wear, and buckles of silver and turquoise. We sat high up in the King's pavilion, among the chieftains, among the judges, with cushions to lean upon,

97

and a wide view of the arena, end to end. And Dio rode just a pace behind the King, on a white pony, carrying the torch high. They made a circuit of the course, while the King's people shouted and sang. Then the King sat watching on his mount at the starting line, and Dio rode round again, this time leading the athletes, all in white robes. I looked out for Peri, and for Philip. There they were, among the throng. Then they retired to the farthest end of the course, and prepared themselves. Most of the runners kept their tunics, but Philip cast off his white garment and made himself almost naked. A scarlet tape was held across the course, in front of the runners. They pressed forward, standing with the tape touching their chests. From his place of honour far behind them Philip crouched, bent nearly double, his arms crooked up against his ribs. Dio and the King were riding now towards the starting tape. The King called out, a loud wild yell. Dio raised the torch, dipped it, and set the flame against the tape. A huge roar rose from the crowd, the tape fell away, the runners charged forward in a thrusting mass. From behind, Philip began to run, smoothly, calmly.

As the runners swept past us I saw how far back Philip was. Much too far. The main body of runners, however, were spacing out now; some were dropping back, there was more room among the leaders. They swept past us and round to the far side of the circuit. Philip gained a little ground. As they came past the pavilion for the second time, Philip overtook some of the stragglers. The King and Dio, returning, took their seats beside the winning post. It was hard to see what was happening on the other side of the circuit. I couldn't pick Philip out. I thought he must have fallen; then, as they swung round on to the last straight, I saw him again, running in a bunch of others. Quarter of a lap ahead of the bunch were four or five, the leading two running shoulder to shoulder, with three others at their heels. 'No one could manage such a handicap,' I said, dreading already the misery and rage that I foresaw would possess the Nikathlon, and make him difficult –

'Look, look!' said Cassie.

And I saw the Nikathlon suddenly emerge from his group, and with an amazing burst of speed, begin to gain ground. His body worked fiercely; every part of him smoothly driving. Sweat shone on him in the bright light. He looked to my astonished stare not like a person, but like a mecho, a marvellous mecho made with uncanny skill, and made for nothing but this, this glorious ferocious drive towards the white tape stretched for the winner. He was running much faster than any of the others, but I still thought it was too far for him; only he was not just going fastest, he was going faster – accelerating as he ran, so that when the leader must have thought it was his race, when three more strides would have given it to him, suddenly Philip shot past him and snatched the victory by a single yard.

Only then did I think to look for Peri, and found him among the cluster of others, just now crossing the line.

The vast crowd cheered and waved. Some young men picked up the Nikathlon where he had fallen to his knees and was gasping for breath, and carried him along shoulder high, bringing him to the foot of the King's throne. I looked down on him, his splendid body glistening, swaying on his perch, his eyes shut, and his face with an expression of rapture, and I was again touched with a cold finger of fear. He seemed to me not human; not because he could run so marvellously, not because of his beauty and strength and skill, but because he could drive himself so; because he could so desire to win. They stood him before the King, and he barely looked at the prizes, the white horse they led to him with a golden bridle, the carpets they were laying at his feet, the carved chest full of silver with the clasped lid thrown open for his gaze. Had he known it would kill him to run so, he would still have done it, and the only prize he cared for was the touch of the unbroken tape across his ribs . . .

When he looked up he looked at Dio. Dio was standing smiling, holding the torch.

They are mad, I thought. That thing has stolen them out of themselves. It doesn't get me. It's only a mecho. An engineer made it in the Ago, just like making shoes or spades. I'm not freaking out for it. And I left. I walked through the shouting, waving crowd, climbed down from the King's pavilion, and made my way through the deserted palace to the room the King had given us.

There I lay down alone, and glad to be.

With the dusk came voices, the sounds of crowds returning, music, the feasting in the halls below. Niko came for me first. 'Come and see, Cal,' he said. 'They've given Philip a special chair, and lots and lots to eat . . .' His face was bright with interest. When I shook my head he shrugged in disbelief, and ran off.

Later Cassie came and sat down quietly. 'Aren't you hungry?' she said. 'I've brought you some figs.'

While I was eating them, Dio arrived. 'What's the matter with you two?' he asked. 'There's a tremendous feast going on.'

'I felt like resting, that's all,' I said.

'Oh Cal,' he said, suddenly extending a hand towards me, 'do come down. This is our place; I think it may be the place. Where the torch belongs . . .'

'No, it isn't,' said Cassie.

'Today everything went right,' he said.

'Yes, but . . .'

'What more do we want?'

'It can't be the kind of thing the old man told us about at

Skiados, can it?' she said, obstinately. 'Philip got all those prizes – real things. The race the torch was made for didn't have a prize – don't you remember? Only a garland that faded in a day.'

'Perhaps they've added the prizes,' he said, visibly shaken. 'That old village elder can't know everything . . .'

'Why don't you ask the King if they ever had a torch here, long ago?' she said.

'Because while the torch burns clear, I am content,' he said.

Eleven

The next day dawned with an iron brightness burning on the face of the desert as before. The people thronged to the cursus, but they were quieter. The King seemed preoccupied, his chieftains nervous. We all sat together in places of honour, and once again Dio rode down to the starting point to burn through the tape with the magic fire of the torch, though this time he went alone, and the King sat in his pavilion. A vast throng of runners were massed behind the tape, more than could possibly run freely, even in so large a space. And as Dio rode towards them the torch flickered and went out. We saw him tilt his head to blow on it, as though to fan the flame, we saw him shake it gently . . .

'I knew, I knew it wasn't meant for here . . .' Cassie said softly, beside me.

Dio must have cut the tape, for it fell away. And the race began. An anxious muttering from the crowds took the place of the cheers of yesterday; people craned and pushed desperately to see. It was hard to see. So many running . . . As the leaders came on to the final straight the winning tape was lifted high, and the leaders ran under it. Then suddenly it was lowered, to groans of anguish from the onlookers and scattered wailing from women in the mass of people, and the runners in front of whom it descended stopped and huddled together, instead of running through it. I turned to ask what was happening, and the question died on my lips as I saw the King sitting slumped, with his cloak drawn over his face. 'One of the King's sons is a youngest son,' whispered a courtier, behind me. 'He did not manage to cross the tape.'

'Is it a disgrace?' I asked, but the man whispered, 'Fatal!'

'Where's Dio?' said Peri suddenly. 'Didn't he come back?' His seat beside the King was empty.

At the same moment we saw Dio – being pushed and knocked, and shrieked at by a crowd of onlookers who had invaded the arena and were trying to reach the group of runners rounded up behind the tape – and the Twaag came bounding up the steps towards us, shouting, 'Get the King to help him! They're blaming him!'

Peri shouldered past the bodyguard, and tugged at the King's robe, his pleading lost in the uproar.

'Blaming him for what, Twaag?' I said, bewildered. Cassie, I noticed, was trembling, as though in the burning light she could be cold. 'They are saying the torch went out and put a curse on the runners . . . made them lose . . .'

The King suddenly stood up, threw off his cloak and with a click of his fingers had a blast blown on a horn, which brought a sudden hush. He shouted at the mob before him. With an angry muttering they thrust Dio to the front, and pushed him on to the steps at the foot of the throne. Dio had a cut on his cheek and seemed unsteady on his feet, but he turned round at once to the crowd and said, 'Give me the torch back.'

A roar of rage answered him. Then he was seized by two of the King's bodyguard and led swiftly away, behind the awnings of the pavilion, struggling and shouting for the torch as he went. Hands were laid on us also, commanding hands, leading us away swiftly and insistently. We went down byways, slipping and struggling through lanes knee-deep in sand where nobody had cleared a path, and came to a strange domed building like a beehive, without windows, and with one huge door, into which we were thrust, and shut in, in the dark.

Very slowly our eyes accustomed themselves. There was an opening at the height of the dome above us, which let in a tiny column of light. It was nearly cool, and once we began to get used to the contrast from the heat outside it was pleasant. On a shelf at one side was a water-jar and a dipper. We drank, and I tore a strip from my cloak and washed Dio's scratches and cuts. We had all been shaking from shock when they first closed the door on us; now we slowly calmed down. I crept round, making sure that each of us in turn was all right. Niko was sucking his thumb, curled up beside the urchin, saying, 'I wish I had Mela here.' I hugged him. The urchin grinned up at me. 'We don't have no time to be bored, much . . .' he said.

Peri and I were untouched; Cassie was still shaking.

'It just suddenly went out, without warning, the same as it did at Palcastra,' Dio said.

'And for the same reason?' I wondered, aloud.

'Surely they can't massacre all those who got past the tape,' said Peri. 'There were dozens of them! I don't believe it.'

'Something feels terrible,' said Cassie.

'If only it would give us some warning,' said Dio. 'If only we knew when it was going to do that. Sooner or later it will get us into terrible trouble . . .'

'Sooner or later?' said Peri incredulous. 'What do you call this? How much more trouble do you want?'

I sat down, leaning against the foot of the wall to wait.

The King came in with lanterns. His household servants thronged the chamber, and hung the lamps on iron brackets in the walls. I thought: We shall be comdemned. He will judge us for the insult, for the omen, because the torch would not bless the race of the younger sons. I remembered that on the island the penalty had been death, though we had escaped the intended fate.

But what happened utterly surprised me. Dio leapt to his feet and sprang to the centre of the chamber. A column of light suddenly stood through the gloom of the dome, so that I realized the abrupt dawn of the desert was blazing outside. Dancing motes of dust seethed in the pillar of light, and it cloaked Dio in brightness – brighter far than the torches – and blazed in his hair, crowning him with a halo of light.

'You have deceived us!' Dio said, with a great force of rage in his voice. 'What have you kept from us? Why did the torch go out?'

'I might have thought to ask you that,' said the King.

'But you know the answer, and you know that I do not. What evil were you working yesterday? Something foul enough to put out the light we brought to you, and shameful enough for you to keep it hidden from me when you asked me to start the race. But the torch is not deceived, as you saw. Now what have you to say to us?'

And the King answered him, meekly. I stared, and felt again the familiar chill of fright. Dio? Who should have gone home and planted olives and now stood blazing, wearing the morning like a garment, and calling a king to account . . .

'I have taken all night, and needed all my authority, to seek out your torch from those who seized it,' the King said, 'and to bring it back to you.' He gestured, and one of his servants brought the torch forward, and laid it at Dio's feet on a scarlet cloth. It was battered and crushed. The beautiful chased and embossed patterns with which the metal cone was covered were dented and deformed, and it was no longer cylindrical, but flattened. The rim was cracked in several places.

Dio looked down at it, and tears sprang to his eyes and glinted on his cheeks. The bar of light in which he was standing cast his eyes into deep shadow, but brightly sparkled in his tears.

'I am sorry,' the King said. 'My people were disgraced in treating a stranger so. We keep strangers far away, usually, and perhaps you see why.'

'I see nothing,' Dio said, 'except that something evil was involved in that race. What will you do with the winners?'

'The winners?' said the King, in surprise. 'The winners are admitted to the ranks of the tribe. They prosper.'

'The losers, then. What of them?'

'I would like you to understand that I have not invented this,' said the King. 'None of the customs of my people was invented by me, or by anyone within the scope of memory. Our customs come to us down the numberless years. The desert taught us how to survive. The desert is harsh . . .'

'What of the losers?'

'The tribes have too many children. More than a desert living can support. Nor can we carry on our long treks for water and trade any weak tribesman, any who are clumsy, injured, incapable . . . you must see that. Only the most magnificent men, the strongest, finest, can live as we live.'

'So what becomes of the rest?'

'They are dead.'

'Better if they were dead, you mean, so terrible is their fate?'

'No. Worse. Those who lost will be – have already been – put to death. They are taken to a remote and unvisited valley of sand, far out in the desert acres, and there buried in the avalanching dunes.'

There was a silence. I shuddered, remembering the place of bones in which the Twaag had found us.

'And does nobody resist you in this disgusting act?' said Dio coldly. 'Does it take the torch from far away to show you that you commit a crime?'

'The punishment for resisting, for escaping, is terrible,' said the King softly. 'Nobody dares . . . and then it is true that it is necessary. We all know that, as people from the rainy lands cannot know . . .' Then he went on even more softly, 'But I in my weakness, having means that others lack . . . pity me, Torch-bearer. Forgive me, and help me . . .'

'How can you ask for help when you have put out the torch?' said Dio.

But Cassie said, 'Wait, Dio. Ask him what he means.'

The King sat down, drew his cloak across his bowed face, and spoke from behind it. 'I have many sons,' he said. 'One – the youngest of all – was born twisted, and grew limping. But he is brave with it. The tents are full of his laughter and tricks. He is the only child of his mother, and her happiness is dear to me . . .'

'But if he was among the losers in the race of the younger sons, he is already dead,' said Dio.

The King gestured, still bowed beneath his cloak. Two of his bodyguard carried forward a bundle of carpets that they had laid down in the shadows when they first came in. Then one of them stooped, and pulled the fringes of the bundle, so that it unrolled towards Dio, and laid at his feet, in the uncanny disc of daylight in which he stood, a young boy, wearing nothing but a runner's long loose shirt.

'I am at your mercy,' the King said, uncovering his face. 'I have rescued my own child. But if this were known, the families of the others would contrive to murder me. I would have not a friend among my people, although I have governed them well.'

The boy dragged himself into a kneeling position on the carpets, and gently circled Dio's legs with his arms, staying for a moment or two before drawing back.

'We are likewise at your mercy,' said Dio at last. 'Why should you scruple to kill us, when you will kill your own?'

'It is always murder to kill strangers,' said the King.

Dio shook his head. 'How then can we help you?'

The King stood up. He seemed to have regained his authority. 'I am going to send you out of the desert,' he said. 'I must send you in secret; the families of the losers are all convinced your torch set a curse on their runners, and you cannot be safe here. The people are howling for your blood. I am sending you away in darkest secret; so if you would, you could take Ahmet with you, you could take him into another country, where he can find some way to live. He will be lost to us for ever, and yet I shall be able to say to his mother, "The rising sun yet shines upon him, far off . . ."'

'This will be but the death of the younger sons, in another way,' said Dio, speaking now to Ahmet. 'If your father sends us into the desert we shall perish there . . .'

'I cannot blame you for that dark thought,' said the King. 'And there will be a risk; if any of my people suspect it; if anyone – worst of all the advizier – sees that Ahmet was not among the sons in the sand-burial, and thinks, "Where, then, is he? Who has left the city early?" There will be danger. But I will give you a guide. I will send one with you who does not get lost in the desert; who knows the water-holes, and the invisible roads in the sands. When he returns with news of your safety, I will reward him very greatly.'

'And if we will not take Ahmet, what then?' said Dio, as if considering.

'I will send you to safety in the way I have promised,' the King said. 'And my son will die. I will kill him now, by my own hand, and bury him secretly. And I will say in my heart, I asked mercy of a son who has no father, of a father who thinks to have no son.'

For a moment I thought the King had said the wrong thing. I remembered Dio's father, standing on the marble fields, shouting, saying under his breath that he would flog Dio when he caught him . . .

Then Dio said, 'I am a son with a mother. Tell Ahmet's

mother that he will be safe with us as long as any of us is safe.'

The King nodded. He laid a hand on his son's head, and said to Dio, 'After nightfall, then; someone will come for you. Do whatever he tells you. And may no one follow you. *Inshallah.*'

He strode away. We heard the door latch bolted behind him, and we sat down, eight of us now, to wait.

And I had time to wonder about Dio. How had he learnt to say the things he said? What an answer he had made to the King! But wasn't he only Dio, who had grown up in our poor and narrow village, three doors from my door, and had known nothing, and expected nothing, and thought to plant olives and keep a goat, and have me carrying the water from the well, and making cheese, and working a loom? I felt a great weight of grief for that Dio, as though he had been someone who had set out with us, and whom we had deserted; lost, left abandoned, somewhere along the way. And I knew that if we went back looking for him we would find him dead. But I remembered him; I had not been afraid to marry him, it was the old man of whom I had been afraid.

Twelve

In the dead of night someone unlatched the door. Outside, the sharp chill of the desert night was full of muted sounds of movement; the velvet *Hurrumph* of a horse snorting quietly, small tinklings of bridle and harness, the silken sounds of hoof and footfall in the sand. The Twaag's voice said in a hoarse whisper, 'Come out; make no sound.'

I got up and groped my way blindly through the door, colliding with someone on the way. There was no moon; the stars were brilliant overhead, with the cold radiance that celebrates themselves and shows nothing else. Hands seized me from behind and lifted me off my feet, so that I squeaked with fright, but they only lifted me on to the saddle of a crouching camel, and guided my flailing hands to rest on the pommel and hold fast. My knees were wedged against bulging saddle-bags. Then the camel lurched to its feet, nearly throwing me off balance, and we set off.

Riding a camel, I soon found, was like wallowing in a rudderless boat, pitching and yawing on the mindless waters of the sea, the smell of beast, flesh and fur and dung, replacing the bleak tang of salt.

At first we were crossing the city; taking turns through the sandy streets, passing now and then a window dimly lit from within, and once a watchman, fast asleep in the glow from a dying lamp. We were a creaking of saddle leather, hushed feet and held breath, passing as a crowd of grotesque shadows cast on the opposite wall. I could not discern us, neither count nor distinguish, before we had passed the faint lamplight into the utter darkness again.

I don't know when we went through the city gate; I heard no voices, no struggle, only some sixth sense telling me we were now in the open again, on the wide face of the featureless sands. Then shortly a voice said loudly, 'We must move fast, now! Yea! yea!' and the camel-keepers cracked their rods. My own mount speeded up. Then a moment came when I could just make out the shapes of camels and riders ahead of me, and saw that my camel was being led by a man walking rapidly beside me. On my left, outlined against the earliest lightening of the dawn sky, was the Nikathlon, on camel-back, leading his horse. Then the rim of the sun just surfaced above the distant dunes, and we could see. We still rode onwards for some time, while the glare and heat of the sun gradually intensified, until the heat was unbearable. I was nearly fainting with the weight of the heat on my uncovered head, the burning of the light on my eyes, when at last a halt was called. We moved a little to one side of the line of advance we had been taking, and the tribesmen with us unrolled a black tent and put it up on long poles. We crept into the shade it provided. I looked around and said at once, 'Where is the Twaag?'

'That's funny,' said Peri. 'He was with us; I heard him.' And we looked with dire suspicion at the stranger from whom the tribesmen had taken the order to stop. He grinned at us. He had a craggy face, with a large mouth. Then he covered his face up to the eyes, drawing a fold of his head-dress across, and we all saw at once that he was the Twaag. He laughed. 'My own brother would not know me with my face bared,' he said, letting the cloth fall, and showing us again his unfamiliar features. 'This is the best disguise . . .'

'And you need disguise?' asked Dio.

'If I am to slip back unnoticed; if the King's honour is to be untarnished . . .'

I was listening, but through veils of drowsiness, and before the buzz of voices had died down I was fast asleep.

I woke when someone stepping over me let the edge of a garment trail lightly across my face. For a moment I lay looking up at the texture of the heavy tent-cloth all thinned and shot through with blazing light. Then I turned my head, saw that it was the Twaag who had moved past me, and got up to join him. He was shading his eyes and staring fixedly at the horizon.

Disorientated by sleep, I did not realize at first that he was looking back the way we had come. 'Wake the others,' he said to me. 'Let's move on.'

And he kept us moving well into the night. We stopped only to pass round water-bottles, and share handfuls of bread and dates, so that I became sure the Twaag had seen something behind us. But I was riding next to Ahmet, and swiftly found he spoke no English, or feigned to speak none, and could answer questions only with smiles. Most of his smiles were directed at Cassie, who rode humming quietly under her breath. For whatever reason, we were moving as fast as our beasts could carry us, and the Twaag was riding in the rear. The moon was setting before he let us stop to sleep. Then he woke us at first light, and beckoned us out of the tent. 'Look there,' he said. He pointed at the horizon, glowing with a band of lemon-yellow light.

'I don't see anything, Twaag,' said Dio.

'Just there – do you see that blur of light? That smudge of mist on the skyline?'

'So?'

'Someone is following us. The dust they raise rises high enough to catch the light, high enough for us to see. They think they are invisible, but in this light I can see them.'

'Could it just be someone making a desert crossing – someone who just happens to be behind us?'

The Twaag shook his head. 'This is not a common route I bring you. And if they meant no harm they would show themselves; they would overtake us in full view. We are going very slowly.'

'Why are we going slowly?' I asked him. 'Isn't this as fast as we can?'

'We carry too much. We are leading horses, we have put heavy loads on the camels. Those who pursue us certainly travel light.'

'Then we too should travel light,' said Dio. 'Why are we laden?'

'We have what Ahmet will need to keep a prince's rank in some coastal princedom; we have the Nikathlon's prizes . . .'

'We must abandon them,' said Dio.

'And your torch with them?' said the Twaag.

'No,' said Dio, 'not that.'

'Anyway, that's not heavy,' piped up the urchin. 'We don't even know what bag it's in . . .'

'I think we must turn aside from the shortest route to the coast and visit a water-hole,' said the Twaag. 'Perhaps there is a way round this . . .'

Without him, of course, we wouldn't have known we were turning aside . . . the desert was all a featureless waste to us.

I had supposed that a water-hole would be just a hole in the ground, like the place where the Twaag, when he first met us, had dug in to replenish the drinking-bottles. So that when we saw it, it took my breath away. We came over a crest of the dunes and saw below us and a little way off a grove of palm trees, towering trees, their arched and delicate fronds held high into the sky, and all of a deep and glossy green. Below them in scattered patches of blazing emerald little fields lay suddenly growing, between the stony apricot-gold sand and a mud wall which ringed it all round. Outside the wall, among the tiny brilliant fields, grew prickly stunted trees, among which a few goats were grazing in the care of little dark-robed boys.

When we came over the brow of the rise and looked down on this scene, the Twaag reined in his camel and we halted for a moment. The goat-boys ran up to us, calling to him, wild with excitement. 'Le chef de caravan est içi!' they were saying; something like that; they weren't words I knew. But the Twaag looked pleased. 'It's all right,' he said. 'T'hami is here.'

Then he beckoned Philip to come up beside him. 'Nikathlon,' he said, 'is there anything among those prizes which you want to keep? I am going to rid us of most of them, including the horse. But keep something back, if you like.'

The Nikathlon appeared affronted. 'Do what you like with them,' he said. 'I don't care.'

The Twaag said, 'You strove immensely to win them, friend.'

'I strove to win,' said Philip. 'And I did win. How will you rid me of that?'

The Twaag shrugged. He exchanged a few words with Ahmet in the desert tongue, and then instructed us. We all rode suddenly and swiftly down from the brow of the hill, and through a cracked and eroded mud gateway into the settlement.

We were in a warren of little lanes, running between mud walls. And we were in shade! The lovely palms stretched their arching, frondy branches between us and the glaring sun. Water ran about in narrow shallow channels lined with smoothed mud, controlled by little wooden paddles, taking every drop of it where it was wanted. Tugging at my shoe, as

I rode my camel single file behind the others, a child pointed out to me the black tents under the palms in a grove beside the path, and said, awed, wide-eyed, 'Le chef de caravan!' But we rode into a dusty open space, ringed round by mud walls and deep-blue doors, and halted.

Once there we raised our tent and spread our rugs, and made a pile of the bulging saddle-bags in the middle of the tent floor. The Twaag stood at the tent door and waited. Soon three men appeared, strangely dressed in rust-red with black head-dresses, and they sat down among us. And then talk went on and on, in the desert tongue. One object after another was unpacked from the saddle-bags and displayed; talk continued. We got up one by one and slipped away to wander under the palms, and to look at the miraculous water. It bubbled up from under a red rock and ran into a stone basin, from which every single drop was led away in tiny channels to the fields. But in the basin it made a deep pool, in which the little boys of the settlement were splashing, naked, and in which we too swam, hugging our wet clothes to our bodies for the welcome chill afterwards. When the Twaag at last called us back to him the saddle-bags had shrunk; only the water-bottles and the food-bags were intact. Our camels were grazing and drinking among the others, and the three grizzled men had gone. The Twaag put down two leather purses, one in front of Philip, one in front of Ahmet. 'This is what I could get,' he said. Philip picked his up, and it jangled. He loosed the thong, and out fell a cascade of metal buttons, some silver, some gold. I reached out curiously, and took one between finger and thumb. It had no holes in it.

'What are they?' I asked. 'What use are they?'

'No use,' said the Twaag. 'But the coast people trade with them. When we reach the coast you will be able to exchange them for things like those we traded for them here – horses, clothes, weapons. We can carry them easily. Meanwhile I have traded for better mounts. When darkness comes, we will ride away very fast.' Then he turned to Ahmet, who was dejectedly jingling his share of the buttons in his closed purse. He smiled at the boy, and brought out from a fold of his robe a funny square board made of cedar-wood, with square lines inset on it in gleaming mother-of-pearl. Ahmet shouted with joy, and, sitting down with the board in front of him, called to Cassie and Niko, and began to show them how to play. We gathered a circle of watchers, boys, and old men, and shy little girls wearing red clothes all covered with silver sequins and blue embroidery, and people began to lay bets on the game. Later they gave us food – dark, tacky stew served under pointed hats of heavy clay, and full of little bitter almonds and chewy fruits. We ate, and laughed, and said 'thank you' in sign language, and played on. So we spent the evening of the day in the oasis at nine-men's-morris, using golden discs for counters, and losing some of them in the sand.

At nightfall we moved on. We rode all night, going rapidly on fresh mounts, and by dawn we were far away. But still the Twaag saw something that troubled him on the horizon in the south. We took only a short rest at mid-day, and rode on. In the middle of the second night on from the water-hole, the stars above our heads began to fade, and go out. It was quite sudden; we were riding under the usual spectacular display, heights above heights of icy sparks glittering, and then we were in unbroken darkness, as though we had ridden under a roof. 'What is it?' said Cassie, calling to the Twaag.

I thought the air smelt different, and was stirring out of its usual deathly stillness.

'Clouds,' said the Twaag. 'It's going to rain! That's all we need. Even I begin to wonder if that torch is cursed indeed . . .'

'Why does it matter if it rains?' I asked him.

'When the sand is wet it holds footprints,' he said.

'And are you sure someone is following us?'

'Yes.'

'What do they want?'

'Nothing but harm, I'm certain; exactly what, I'm not sure.'

'But what could it be?'

'Three things. Perhaps they want Ahmet, to kill him, as they believe he should have been killed. As I believe, also, though I will try to stop them.'

'But, Twaag, how could you believe . . .' I said.

'This loser is a king's son. But to some father every loser was a prince . . .'

I thought that over. Somehow it didn't add up. Of course it was unfair to save one person . . . but wasn't it better than not saving anyone? 'What else could they want?' I persisted.

'They could want Ahmet to return him alive to the tribes, and thus disgrace the King. If it is that, it means revolt. I too would lose everything, I would share the disgrace.'

'And the third thing?'

'They could want to take the torch. They were fighting over whether to keep it as a weapon for cursing enemies, or whether to bury it deep in the place of bones to rid themselves of its power. The King had great difficulty getting it back, and the people were sullen and angry with him over it.'

I rode on, thinking. It seemed to me much the most likely thing they wanted was the torch. I wondered if Dio would give it up easily, now that it was broken and put out. And I knew at once that he wouldn't; he would die first.

The dawn broke, and showed us, luridly lit from below, the underbelly of huge, massed storm-clouds; and then it began to rain. Not normal rain; but slow-falling heavy drops, few and reluctant, followed suddenly by a fierce downpour.

We had a hard time getting the tent up in the downbeat of the torrents of water; when we got under cover we were already soaked to the skin. I remembered for the first time in weeks that it was unpleasant to be cold.

It rained all night. And all the next day. The Twaag thought we were best off staying put, resting the camels, keeping dry. He thought our pursuers would do the same; but if they were still riding, the most likely thing to happen was that they would ride past us; in the rain they would be able to see only a few yards, not the endless vistas presented by the desert under a clear sky. So we remained, huddled together under black canvas weighed down towards our heads by a rainpool, and noisy with rain.

Of course, hedged up close together like that we talked. Dio asked Cassie if she thought the Twaag was right; was there really a pursuit? She nodded, glumly.

Later Peri asked, 'Dio, was the torch badly damaged? Can we look at it?'

'It was already out when they snatched it,' said Dio, his voice heavy with misery.

'But as we know, it can re-light itself . . .'

'The man on the ship said, hold it upside down,' said Niko.

Dio reached out, and patted Niko's shoulder. 'It has been upside down in my pack all this while,' he said. 'The engineer must have been wrong.'

'Dio, listen to me,' said Peri, suddenly sounding urgent. 'We can't go on like this; we've got to try to understand it. It puts us all in danger when it suddenly goes out like that. And we don't expect it; we are taken by surprise. And then we don't know what to do that might make it light up again. Instead of sitting around gloomily like that, help us understand it. We've got to; we've got to *think*.'

'How can we hope to understand it if the engineer couldn't?' he said.

'No – not that kind of understand. Our kind. It's been apparently out, and then it's lit up again; can we think of anything that makes it light? Don't you see? If we knew what it liked, we could look after it better – we could make sure it could light up again. If we knew what puts it out we could keep it safe . . .'

'All right,' said Dio. 'The first time it re-lit we were in the boat, freezing.'

'It saved us,' said Niko. 'It warmed up to save us.'

'But the second time was on the ship, and we didn't need saving,' said Peri.

'P'r'aps it wasn't really out that time,' said the urchin. 'P'r'aps the sea wetted it a bit, but it wasn't really out . . .'

'How could it not have been out?' I asked. 'Fire does go out when you put it in water.'

'Well, but this isn't ordinary fire, though. Ordinary fire doesn't flare up again later,' said Peri.

'What were we talking about when it re-lit those times?' said Dio, warming to the question. 'And what about the time you took it, Cal, and brought it back working again? Were you saying anything that we might have been saying the other times?'

'I wasn't saying anything,' I said. 'None of us were. We were all listening to this old man because nobody else was. We were sorry for him.'

'Is that it? Does it like us to feel sorry for someone? Or kind? Who can remember what we were talking about in that awful boat?'

'I can,' said Cassie. 'The first time was when we were trying to talk the Nikathlon out of jumping over the side; the second time was when the urchin was calling us crazy.'

'What for?' asked Dio. 'What did you call us crazy for?'

'Effed if I remember!' said the urchin. 'Might of bin anything. Most of what goes on with you lot is crazy, in't it?'

'I suppose you were being kind, when you listened to the poet . . .' said Dio.

'But perhaps it wasn't what *we* were doing at all,' said Cassie. 'It might have been what he was doing . . .'

'But he wasn't there the other times, Cassie,' said Dio.

'Yes, but . . .' she broke off. All our tries at thinking about it were like that; they ran off into unfinished sentences, and bafflement.

Towards evening the rain ceased, and the Twaag got us on the move again. He took us further into the trackless waste, hoping that if our stop had given any advantage to our pursuers he might throw them off. I think none of us entirely believed in the pursuit, except Ahmet, and, so she said, Cassie; but the nervousness and constant watchfulness of the Twaag were slowly convincing us. After all, they were the ones who would know best.

As had become usual with us we rode all night, and into the dawn. And at dawn we saw ahead of us an astonishing sight. The sands were suffused with a glowing pink; I thought it was the flush of dawn, but it was not, though the lovely warm radiance of the early light deepened the glow. Ahead of us the desert sands were covered with flowers. From whorls of spiky, stripey leaves slender stems rose, carrying bell-like flowers in every shade of pink and rose. And in the rapidly growing heat that came with morning a faint, faint, delectable fragrance came off the field of flowers, like something remembered rather than real, and beautiful. We all reined in our mounts, and sat there staring. 'Oh, Twaag, Twaag, what is it?' said Cassie.

Even the Twaag sounded awed. 'It is the hundred-year aloe,' he said, 'which flowers after rain . . .'

'Is it everywhere?' I asked.

'Oh, no,' he said. 'Very rare, very few places. I have heard about it; I know that it only lasts one day, and then dies . . .

You cannot see where it will come, it vanishes in the sand
. . . but in another hundred years or so . . . I have never seen
it before . . .'

'Oh, Twaag, and aren't you glad!' said Cassie, laughing
delightedly.

'Allah blesses me in the sight,' said the Twaag solemnly,
'but now we must ride on.'

'Not across the flowers,' I said.

'We'll trample them things if we ride on them,' the urchin
observed.

The Twaag shrugged. 'But by tonight they will die
anyway. And nobody sees them; nobody comes here. Only
because we are driven off the track do we come here . . .'

And I wondered again what had got into us. We who had
let our goats devour the flowers of home . . . but then those
flowers came thick and predictable every season of our lives,
and these were impossible, surviving the impossible shifting
sand, waiting for rain which might take a hundred years to
come.

'Let's ride round them,' said Dio.

'They grow far,' said the Twaag. 'We will lose time, and
those who come after us will ride right through them,
anyway.'

'Then that will be what they do,' said Dio. 'But we will
ride round.'

The Twaag looked anxiously at Ahmet, and translated for
him. And the boy smiled radiantly at Dio, and signed agree-
ment. So we turned, and began to ride round the edge of the
flowers, sweeping for miles across the rolling dunes. Dio
was riding ahead, abreast of the Twaag, and I was just
behind him. So when his saddle-bag began to smell scorched,
the acrid scent reached me. Burning? I looked around wildly,
and then saw that the smoke trailing in the still air came
from Dio's bags. I cried out, yelling to him, and as I did so a

flame licked through the scorched carpet of the bag and the torch fell out, burning brightly, and lay flickering on its side in the sand.

In a moment we were all dancing round and laughing, breathing the heady perfume of the aloes, and full of childlike joy. Dio pranced, holding the torch aloft and laughing like a madman. Then, as we remounted and moved off again, he said, 'But what about that time? Nobody was being kind to anybody, were they? Nobody was saying anything . . . I don't see it; I don't see *anything* the same . . .'

'I think I do,' said Cassie softly; but when I turned to her at once and questioned her, she would only shake her head.

Our enemies caught up with us at the height of the day, while we were lying drowsing and suffering in the heat, under our thin black awning.

There were shouts, screams of alarm. The tent was torn down, and we were flinching and rolling out of the way of a storm of hooves, a stampede as they rode us down. Our bags were tossed about, lances ripped the cloth, they whooped and yelled, and pushed and dragged us about, their nasty curved knives gleaming at our throats. We rose from sleep into the chaos of noise and flailing movement, and danger, and could not grasp what was happening. I saw the Twaag struck down by a man on camel-back and fall with a bleeding forehead, I heard Cassie wailing as someone lifted her up and then dropped her on her back across the baggage. The Twaag was on his feet again, looking around wildly – I supposed for Ahmet. Dio was groping about, calling us by our names. The storm of sand raised by the furious mêlée blinded us beyond hope of seeing anything.

Then suddenly the thundering of hooves was drawing away from us instead of remaining among us, the drifting sand began to settle, and we could see the skyline where an upswell of the desert looked a little way off; across this glimpse of clarity we saw the galloping forms of our enemies sweeping away, perhaps two dozen of them, in full flight.

'The torch!' said Dio.

'Ahmet!' cried the Twaag.

But the torch had not been taken; through the thinning whirls of the sand as it sank back to the ground the torch glowed with a wide halo, like the sun on a winter morning, still standing where Dio had propped it; and Ahmet had not been taken; Ahmet crawled sheepishly out of a fold of the torn tent-cloth, and answered to his name. We looked around bewildered.

'What, then . . .?' said Peri.

It was the Nikathlon they had taken.

Thirteen

'We could say, "It is the will of Allah"; or we could follow and try to buy him back,' said the Twaag.

'Buy him?' said Dio.

'He will fetch a high price,' said the Twaag.

'They didn't take his purse of counters,' I said. 'I found it a moment ago.'

'That might not be enough,' said the Twaag. 'Those raiders were Hassades. They take and sell slaves. And I should have realized they would want the boy who runs like that; they will take him to the coast, and they will ask a small fortune for him.'

'Because he runs fast?' I asked.

'In the south Province there is wealth won and lost at races; trainers from there buy boys on the coast . . .'

'Then we must buy him first,' said Dio.

'Yes; if we can. Mount, then; we must follow them.'

And when I gave Dio Philip's jangling purse, which I had picked up from the sand, Ahmet was beside me, giving his too into Dio's keeping. The Twaag said something to him in their own tongue, but he took Dio's hand and closed his fingers gently round the thongs of the purse. And I remembered, as we rode, turned as we were from pursued to pursuers in a few chaotic moments, what we had exchanged for the purses: all the bowls and carpets, and the lovely horse and splendid bridle – surely we had wealth abounding in our hands, and could afford to ransom a boy . . .

It was not hard to catch up with the Hassades. There were

perhaps a hundred of them; they did not bother to throw us off the trail, for we could do nothing against them anyway. From time to time we would climb to the crest of a slope and look down on their encampment, and so we caught sight of Philip, far off. They had him in a cage, which travelled slung between two camels, and they gave him exercise when they stopped, running him beside a camel, on the end of a thong tied to his wrist.

We were outraged to see someone kept like that; but the Twaag thought he was being well treated for a slave. 'They won't harm a hair of his head; they'll feed him like a prince, they'll run him for an hour a day,' he said. 'They won't damage the value of their loot.'

But Cassie and I, talking in whispers while we rested, fretted about him. 'Do you remember him in the boat?' she asked me, 'talking about throwing himself in? He gets dejected so easily . . .'

'We ought to tell him we are still nearby; that we will rescue him . . .'

And without telling the others we simply walked the short space that separated our noonday rest from the fringe of the Hassades' camp, and walked up to the cage in which Philip was lying. A sleepy guard seemed not to care, or perhaps did not know we were not of his own party; anyhow, he let us whisper to Philip for a few moments before rousing himself to chase us off.

We thought we had cheered him; we had even won a brief smile from him, but Dio was angry with us when we returned. 'You might have been taken too; and then we would have had three to worry about!' he said.

'Not likely they take girls,' said the Twaag. 'Girls no good to sell.'

Dio stubbornly made us promise not to wander off again. Cassie went to lie down beside Niko, and Dio lectured me.

'I didn't even know you liked him, Cal,' he said. 'I know he likes you. He thinks you could run, if he taught you.'

'I don't like him,' I said. 'He's horrible and selfish and cold. And I don't want to learn to run. But he's with us; and he isn't strong . . . I was afraid for him . . .'

'Isn't strong? Whatever do you mean? He can run, and jump, and . . .'

'In his mind, not his body. He only wants glory, winning. The moment that turns sour in some way he's ready to drown, or give up . . . he isn't tough, Dio, not like you.'

'Not like me?'

'Not like you used to be. You are a bit like him now, sometimes, fine as long as that thing is burning, and in black despair if it goes out . . .'

'How can I help that? Can't you see what it feels like to be leading all of you I don't know where, if it goes out and leaves us?'

'Can't you see that when it goes out we need you most of all — that's when we really need a leader?'

'Seeing that, and being able to do it, are far apart . . .' he said. 'I'm scared quite a lot of the time now, Cal. Aren't you?'

'I'm all right while you're all right. I panic when you go gloomy.'

'Do you ever wish we had run back to the village instead of helping the old man?' he asked. 'We'd be at home now; we wouldn't have anything to worry about, because they wouldn't let us decide anything for ourselves anyway . . .'

'But we couldn't have done that. I wouldn't have let a goat lie like that, dying . . . It's no use wishing we had done something we *couldn't* have done.'

'That's what I think, too,' he said. 'I'm glad you agree. Cal? You know, I like the things you think. I'm glad to be with you . . .' He reached out, and gently touched my hand.

126

A little flame of joy leapt within me, but I said, 'You don't have to say that kind of thing. I know how it is . . .' and then he turned away.

We came to a range of snow-covered mountains, so like the heights of home they made our hearts ache; and the pass was craggy and difficult, and the camels had to be led, not ridden. In the clefts and high valleys of these mountains little pink-washed villages clung to the slopes, and there must have been rainfall, for there were tiny terraced fields of red and golden earth, and almond trees, and date palms growing in the bottom of gorges beside sluggish red streams. Beyond, we were in another country, a dry and stony plain, with oases on it here and there; with villages, and towns with domes, and narrow tall towers, and bustling people. We bought food in the village markets, and heard reports of the slavers, who were only hours ahead of us; our water-bottles we could fill free at cool, clean wells.

When the Hassades reached their destination it was a shore; a sand bar made a harbour, and there was a little stone quay, and dozens of boats at anchor. Behind the shore was a flat level, ringed with a crumbling mud wall and trodden bare of grass, and here the market was in progress. The Hassades set up their tents, displayed their captives tied together in rows, and prepared to do business. The market was seething with people. Up against the wall at one end were camels, and in another corner sheep and goats. Meat was being butchered in strange pieces – goats' heads with fur and horns complete, whole legs with hooves still on them, buckets of dark offal. On carpets laid on the ground silver trinkets were spread out to catch the eye, vegetables piled up in the dust beside kitchen pots; there was even a man offering to pull out teeth. He had a string with a running loop at one end, and a donkey on the other – we shivered at the thought. Among the crowds were some folk strangely dressed: neither like the people of our villages in Hellada, nor like the people of the desert, nor even like the farmers of the good lands we had crossed since leaving the desert; but in suits made all in one piece, and of fine shining cloth in bright colours. They stared and chattered, and made notes about the slaves on show. And we had high hopes; we watched boy after boy put up on a platform and auctioned. Their prices were easily within what the Twaag was holding in readiness. But the Nikathlon and some dozen others were not put on sale the first day. Towards the evening of the second day they put a row of cages down and opened them like starting-gates, and shouted to their prisoners to run. Some simply stepped out of their cages and stood, or jogged a few paces. Some ran, as they were told. But Philip set off like an arrow from a bow, like a bird on the wing, and fled across the sandy space, going fast and far, so that they sent a rider on horseback with a net to cast over him and catch him and bring him back. Could he have thought he was running for freedom? Did he think it was really a race and he could win it? But all he achieved was to send his own price soaring far out of our reach.

And within minutes he was out of the market-place, and down to the shore, and on a ship, and the ship was casting moorings to go. Niko, running after him, seeming to play, helping to slip hawsers in rings, managed just to learn from a seaman the name of the port she sailed for; and we watched her dark sails out of sight on the wide sea.

When darkness fell we were sitting together round a fire on the beach, conferring. The Twaag had gone off somewhere. The torch was burning steadily and low, and the dusty light of the bright stars overhead was answered dimly by the sheeny surface of the quiet sea. We were talking, of course, about what to do. Peri said, 'We started the journey without the Nikathlon. We can finish it without him.' And that thought lay in a long pause in our conversation. Then we heard footsteps, and the Twaag came back, bringing with him a stranger, a man of middle age and slender build, wearing desert garments.

'This is Brameen,' the Twaag told us. 'He has been a slave in the Province. He will tell you about it.'

And I knew, when I heard him say, 'He will tell you . . .' and not 'He will tell us . . .', that the Twaag would not go with us; he was turning back.

Brameen said he had been captured from a desert oasis as a boy, and taken to the coast and sold. His master had been a certain Moosyer Tours, who kept a large stable . . .

'A stable?' Dio asked.

In that country, Brameen told us, runners were owned, like horses. Owners kept groups of runners, called 'stables', and raced them against each other, betting huge sums of money on the outcome. He, Brameen, had been kept as a running slave for seven years. Well fed, well exercised, and locked up all the time he was not running.

'How did you escape?' Dio asked him.

Brameen said escape was not possible. A good runner was worth money, and was watched and guarded by stable-boys all the time, night and day. He himself had been freed because he went lame. They turned him off, knowing he could never win again. Brameen had longed to be allowed to go on racing, since he had known no other life; but a lame slave was no good to them, so they had simply opened his stable door and chased him away. Then he had walked home; hundreds of miles to the Rock, and a begged crossing on a ferry-boat . . . he warned us it was idle to think of going after our friend. Helping a slave to escape in the Province was theft, and the penalty for theft was hanging.

'And what are you now?' asked Cassie. 'What has become of you?'

'I am a basket-maker,' Brameen said, 'a trade in which being lame is of no consequence. But I dream of the great crowds roaring as we ran down the straight . . .'

'Perhaps Philip will like it,' said Peri. 'It sounds like his sort of thing.'

'Does anyone like being forced to things?' said Cassie. 'Even Philip?'

And again the question hung in a silence. At last the Twaag said, 'What will you do, now?'

'We will follow, and try to get Philip back,' said Dio.

'Not succeed,' said the Twaag.

'But we will try,' said Dio.

'Perhaps you will hang as thieves,' said the Twaag. 'And then someone bad take the torch. Don't you care about the torch? I thought you were always taking the torch to find races; Brameen say there are good races in the south . . .'

'You mean we should just march away and leave Philip to be a slave?' I said.

'Sometimes things cannot be helped,' said the Twaag. 'And I am thinking of you because you are my friends, because we have been thirsty together, and shared water together. And I think that your torch will not like slave races. I think if you take it near slave races it will go out. And I think that you do not know how to make it light again, and when it goes out you are in trouble. This is why I do not think you should take a ship across to the Rock and go chasing after your runner. You should bow to fate. Many times people must bow to fate. It is not just for you that I say this. A man should accept fate; you should accept it, just as my King should have accepted the race of the younger sons . . .'

'But Ahmet is here,' said Dio. 'And I do not think we can serve the torch by doing things that otherwise . . . I don't think the torch would like to be an excuse; I don't think we can say that we would have tried to help Philip, but that serving the torch prevented us . . . it doesn't work like that, does it, Cassie?'

He turned suddenly to Cassie, asking her as if he thought she knew more than he did. And she answered him quite calmly. 'No.'

'So you will go after him?' said the Twaag sadly.

'Yes,' said Dio, sighing.

'Then this is where our roads part,' the Twaag said. 'I have brought Ahmet to the coastal people, with his purse of money; and I have led you out of the dry land safely. Now I shall go back to my own people. I need to feel parched again, and see the nothingness of sand. My spirit sinks in all this plenty and among so many trees.'

'How shall we do without you?' I said, reaching out towards him.

'If you went south your path and mine would be the same for many miles more,' he said. 'But they could not for ever be the same.'

'I suppose not,' I said sadly. We had come to understand the Twaag, and trust him.

'Brameen will go with you in my place,' the Twaag said suddenly, 'if you will spend a little of the Nikathlon's money to pay him. He will need ten of those coins, now, to provide for his daughter while he goes with you. For that he will lead you to the Province, where the great races are.'

'Can we trust him?' said Dio, looking steadily at the Twaag.

'Could you trust me when first I found you camping on a mound of skulls?' said the Twaag. 'And have I not been your brother, your sister, your mother and your father?'

Dio simply nodded.

'Yet you do not take my advice,' said the Twaag, suddenly grinning. Then he reached out a hand and gently touched the torch, where it stood burning in its bracket beside us.

And touched his own forehead with the fingers that had touched the torch. And wrapped his face again in a fold of his head-dress, so that his own brother would know him a mile away ... And it was only then that he suddenly embraced Ahmet, and shook his head, and we understood that Ahmet would come with us.

When the Twaag had gone Brameen held out his hand, and Dio counted out ten coins on his palm. At once he too strode off into the darkness. We settled down to get what sleep we could.

'Why did he have to run like that?' I asked nobody in particular, scarcely knowing that I spoke the thought aloud.

'He would!' said Dio, feelingly.

'He do rather run first and think later, don't he?' said the urchin, admiringly.

'He didn't know . . .' I said.

'And if he had known?' said Cassie. 'Can you imagine him running slowly?'

We laughed.

'Oh, we'll find him,' said Dio, 'and set him free somehow.'

'Aren't you worried about the torch, Dio?' said Niko. 'Mightn't it go out when it gets to some more rotten races?'

'I think Cassie will help us,' said Dio softly in the dark. 'I think Cassie has guessed how it works. Haven't you, Cassie?'

'Yes, I think so,' she said.

'And you're going to tell us.'

'No,' she said, 'I'm not going to tell you, Dio.'

'Well, not now, anyway,' he said, easily. 'There's no need now . . .' The torch after all was still glowing like a hot coal, comforting us in the darkness.

'Not now, not ever,' she said. 'I can't.'

I sat up abruptly, and stared at her shadowy outline, appalled at her. But Dio, still sounding easy, only said, 'I expect you will when we need it . . .'

Fourteen

In the morning we took ship. Brameen had found us a passage on a vessel carrying dried fruits and painted bowls, that was crossing to a place called Mazarron, from where Brameen told us we would have to walk. It was many weeks' walking, but he could not find a ship going further. And so we found ourselves travelling again in inhabited country in which grew olives and vines and a little corn, like our own land, but lusher; fertile, and watered. And this journey was different. You cannot travel in inhabited country without attracting attention, if you are carrying a burning torch of strange design. First, people began to follow us; they marched with us a little way on the road towards the next village, and when most of them turned back one or two did not . . . over and over again a girl or boy came to one of us and begged to be allowed to join us. Dio tried to refuse them; some took his refusal with blank faces and came anyway. And then rumour began to precede us; little children crowded the outskirts of the settlements and lined the roads, waiting for us. As we passed they joined us, falling in line behind the torch, singing and linking arms. And more and more often a deputation of villagers would be waiting in the squares, or on the steps of the church, and one of us would be required to tell our story and explain the torch.

More and more often it was Peri who told the story; Dio stood silently holding the torch, keeping some mystery about him. Peri got good at it; he never failed to tell how the advizier's men had burnt their hands as the torch threw a red-hot fury at the attempt to wrest it from us; he hinted that it brought luck and power to those who treated it well. Sometimes we had food and a roof to sleep under, and did not pay for them; in some places the little boys ran races round the village for us, the women brought us gifts – bright knitted caps and gloves, and suchlike. In one princely town we were feasted on a sheep roasted in the open air, and the cobbler mended all our shoes. And each morning, it seemed to me, more of us walked on, so that those of us who had set out – how long ago it seemed! – from Olim had become a few among many.

Brameen was worried. And of course he was right; going to mount a secret raid and rescue someone, it is hard to see how a hundred can do as well as a dozen, or a dozen as well as two or three. And yet we couldn't stop people coming with us . . . what we could do was to keep quiet about Philip; tell nobody why we were going to the races in the Province. Let them think simply it was part of our quest for where the torch belonged, although in fact we already knew enough about those races to know that it could not be for them the torch burned on so long, so far from home.

Dio worried about it. Once, as I was walking beside him, he asked me to help him. 'Cassie won't tell me,' he said. 'Do you think she might tell you?'

'Might tell me what?'

'What it is she knows – has guessed – about the torch.'

'I could try. Why won't she tell you?'

'I don't know. Have I offended her, do you think? I know I didn't mean to . . . but I can't understand. And, Cal, you know it isn't just that I'm desperate to know – though I am, I am, because it might help me keep it alight – and it isn't that I think I ought to be the first to know things, since the torch was given to me – though come to that, I don't like to think there's something I don't know . . .' he trailed away into silence, biting his lip.

'But . . .' I prompted him.

'But I thought we were all together in this; that we would always stick together and help each other . . . if suddenly someone won't help, if someone disagrees, think how difficult it might get . . .'

'Do you mean if someone disobeys you, Dio? Because as far as I know I'm the only one that has to do what you say.'

'But do I go around giving orders?' he said. 'Do I throw my weight about? Do I? I didn't order Cassie, I asked her.'

'And she said no.'

'She said no. Help me find out – or at least find out why. And Cal? Cal, I'm not ordering you – just asking you. Right?'

'I'll look for a good moment,' I said.

But a good moment was hard to find. The journey was becoming stranger. Brameen was taking us on a route along the coast – not right along the beaches, for fear of pirates who descended suddenly, he said, and took captives from the roads in sight of the sea, but a mile or two inland, keeping parallel with the coast. Otherwise, Brameen said, we would find a great range of mountains across our path. And we began to pass places full of strangeness – places built in the Ago. We could see at once that these places had changed far more than the land we knew. In our land we had seen nothing like them; I suppose I had never wondered how, or where, the wonder-workers of Ago had lived. I had not thought they would have made huge quays, jutting far into the sea and holding smooth acres of water, enough for whole fleets of ships. Or that they would have levelled roads so wide an army could have marched down them shoulder to shoulder, hundreds at a time. But these things we saw, though there were only little fishing-boats in the harbours and the roadways were under grass.

We came to a place where we were welcomed with food

on tables spread in the shade of the trees of the village square. The children ran races in our honour, competing only for sweetmeats and flowers, and Dio let the winner run a lap of honour all round the village, carrying the torch. Someone's goat was lame and giving no milk, and Cassie and I went up the hillside looking for a herb we knew which we would have given to one of our own goats in such a state, and we found it, and fed it to the poor beast in handfuls of grass, so that the family who owned her were full of goodwill for us.

In such a place I felt suddenly weary of travelling; I thought wistfully how easy it would be for us simply to stop there, and cut another little field out of the hillside, and live as these kind and friendly people lived, in a way we understood. And it was in this place, where we felt welcome and trusting, that they offered to guide us the next day. 'The roads into the hills are dangerous,' said the young man who was offering himself as company. 'You could easily get lost. You might not find him at all.'

'Find who?' asked Dio. 'We were not going into the hills. We were keeping close to the coast. We hope to go between the mountains and the shoreline, into the Province.'

'But we thought you had come to find the scholar . . .' said the young man.

'We have already sent word to him about you,' said the village priest. 'He hides away otherwise, and will not see people. And of course he lives far from any road, in the remote hills.'

'But who is he?' Dio asked. 'And why do you think we have come on his account?'

'He is the scholar,' said the young man. 'He has spent his whole lifetime finding out about Ago. Things of no use to anybody now, but he doesn't care about that; we thought you had come to ask him about your torch . . .'

'We have,' said Dio. 'We didn't know we had, that's all. And we will gladly accept your help in finding him.' And then he suddenly turned to Cassie, and asked her, 'Is this why we have come? Is this why Brameen brought us this way?'

'You ask me things I don't know,' she said.

'But what do you think?'

'I think we should see the scholar.'

And so the next morning, on donkeys lent to us for the ascent, we climbed into the hills.

It was hard going. The path was rough and steep, keeping beside a torrent which fell in fierce waterfalls from pool to pool. Trees overhung the narrow gorge of the stream, and made it hard to follow the rocky banks. We zigzagged up the ascent, and came out at last in a high valley, along the narrow floor of which the stream meandered more quietly. Bare hills soared on either side of the track, and the valley bottom was marshy and spongy under the donkeys' hooves, so that it was easier to ride along the bed of the stream, on the submerged gravel. We rode on, for an hour more. And then the valley opened out, and displayed to us a wide sweep of mountain tops. A lake, nearly perfectly round, like a dish full of reflected sky, spread out ahead of us, and we could see that it was the source of the stream we had been following, which left it under a little bridge of stone with a cunningly made arch. And on the bank of the lake was an Ago place; a building of rose-red stone, tall and complex, with towering arches and a half-broken roof, ruined like a leaf in winter, with stone veins still standing . . . at one end of the building a square tower was still intact, with windows like narrow slits, and even a thin thread of smoke ascending from a makeshift chimney. The door to this tower was a whole storey above the ground, and was reached by a flight of wooden steps with a drawbridge to be crossed at the top.

We could see at once that the scholar would not need to see people if he didn't want to, but he was waiting for us, standing at his high door, surrounded by his view of snow-topped mountains, and looking down at us as we filed round the curving shore of the lake towards him. Before we reached the foot of his siege ladder, he had descended and had come to meet us, his hands held out to us, and with tears in his eyes.

'I did not believe them,' he told us, 'and yet you are true. The torch is really journeying again. Show it to me; may I hold it in my hands?'

Dio gave it to him, unhesitating. I wouldn't have hesitated either; the scholar had a heavily lined face, stamped deeply with an expression of childlike curiosity, of dreamlike thought. White hair chopped roughly short framed his face, and his clothes were homespun and plain. Only his hands showed that his life was different from the villagers' lives; they were pale and delicate, with pearly unbroken nails, papery unsunburnt skin. He took the torch gently, and looked at it admiringly. 'It is more than a thousand miles from Olympia,' he said. 'Oh, further far . . . Come in and sit by my fire, and tell me about the journey, about the journey and the starting of the journey . . . come, come, do!'

'All of us?' said Peri, smiling slightly, looking at the rickety steps and the drawbridge and the crowd of us pressing round – for we were a crowd now, some three dozen, with all who had joined us on the way.

'Sancho will light a fire for us in the great hall,' the scholar said, 'and you shall all come in. There will be wine enough; and bread, probably, and olives. Will that do?'

'Bread, and wine, and olives, and talk!' said Dio, his voice warm and light. 'What princes do as well!'

'A generous guest makes anything a feast,' the scholar said. And we all went in.

His tower was full of books. Books everywhere – in close

ranks, row upon row, on shelves that lined the room from floor to rafters, in piles on floors and tables, in stacks to one side of every tread of the stone stairs, some rotting, some with broken bindings, some intact, all smelling of dust . . . and we were so ignorant he had to show us books, show us that they were made of leaves of paper, dozens, hundreds together, each leaf covered thickly with little signs in code.

'Are they Ago things?' asked Niko, looking round amazed.

'From Ago, and before Ago,' the scholar said. 'Being able to read them kept Ago together . . . kept them knowing what they needed for those wonderful times.'

'What is "read"?' I asked him.

'Understanding the code. Decoding the books.'

'And you can do that?' said Peri. 'Who taught you?'

'I taught myself,' the scholar said. 'At first I had just a few books; the ones the holy men who lived here had left. There was a lot in them about their God, but very little about the world they lived in. But once it got around that I could read, people brought me books. Every book in Spain is here now, I think. People are grateful to me, and they know I want nothing else; they buy any book they see, and repay me with them.'

'Why are they grateful, scholar?' asked Cassie. 'Do you have every one who comes to dinner?'

'The books are powerful,' he said. 'Once, in the vanished world, they showed people how to do the things we have all heard of: how to make pictures fly hundreds of miles, and pull carts without horses – that sort of thing. But even in this dark age they taught me some simple medicine, tricks you might say. Sometimes I have been able to help.'

'Can you make the flying pictures?' said Niko eagerly. 'Can you show us that?'

The scholar shook his head. 'No; but I can tell you why I

can't. If people grasped even that much we would be on the way back . . . as it is, I think we are still on the way down.'

'Tell us that now,' said Niko, taking the scholar's hand. 'I want to know that before supper!'

'In the Ago, then,' he told us, 'nobody could do it; that is, no one person. The pictures shone on frames made of glass. It wasn't any use just throwing the pictures into the sky; there had to be frames ready to receive them. Someone knew how to make the frames; or perhaps each person knew only how to make one part of the frames . . . and that is what we have lost. We can do now what anyone can do alone; or what a few people together, as in a family or a village, can do. But we have lost the art of everything for which the men of Ago worked together, hundreds of them, living far apart from each other. It isn't the knowledge that has gone; or, rather, the knowledge has gone, but the knowledge by itself wouldn't work. We have lost the way of living that made it work . . . you see?'

'Sort of,' said Niko, looking very doubtful.

'That's the trouble, isn't it?' said Cassie. 'All the understanding we have is only sort of . . .'

'You are wise, for a child,' the scholar said. 'The monks who built this tower were keen on wise children – out of the mouths of babes . . .'

Suddenly the scholar's servant appeared in the door. 'Is there to be bread for all these strangers?' he demanded.

'There is, Sancho,' the scholar said. 'Bread, and drink, and a fire in the hall tonight, and straw to sleep on . . .'

'Then I must have help,' Sancho said. 'Are any of them good for anything?'

'Try us,' I said, and Sancho set us to work.

When evening came there was a fire lit in the strange vaulted undercroft of the ruined hall, and bales of straw set

140

round it at a safe distance for us all to sit on comfortably. Bread was baked, and there was a rough but satisfying meal for us. And as we sat down to eat and talk the torch suddenly changed colour, and burned up brightly with a lovely rosy glow, and began to smell sweetly, as though we had cast spices in its flame, though all we had done was set it in a bracket and stand it where it would cast light on the circle of faces.

First we told the scholar about ourselves. Only when we mentioned poor captive Philip were we sad. But the scholar had tears in his eyes while we told him things – how we had lit the torch and how it had burned and been quenched and sprung to life again, and how we had carried it and tried to find its true place . . .

'Why are you crying, scholar?' Cassie asked him. 'Is this a sad story, to your knowing?'

'Oh no, not sad . . .' he said. 'But for me, full of emotion. All the time I've spent reading books, thinking about Ago; all that time I have thought of Ago as gone for ever, extinguished. And yet you bring to me a living spark, however tiny . . . of course I am moved to tears . . .'

'It burns far brighter than a tiny spark tonight,' Dio said. 'It likes it here, scholar. Yours is a good place, though not a place of races . . .'

'The spark I meant is not that of the torch, not in itself,' the scholar said, 'but that impulse in you, Dio, and in your friends that made you take it up and carry it through the world, without understanding what you were doing . . . I suppose you didn't understand?'

'We knew only what the old man told us; and then what the elder in Skiados added. Since then we have often been frightened, and sometimes without any glow from the torch to cheer us. And we have found out nothing more. Unless you can tell us things . . .'

'I can't tell you anything about the torch itself,' the scholar

141

said, tipping his wine-beaker and sipping from it. 'I can tell you something about yourselves, if that's what you wanted to know.'

'How could you know about us?' I asked him.

'I know about your names,' he said. 'Do you want to know about your names?'

'What about them?' said Peri. 'What is there to know about names?'

'Greek names,' the scholar said. 'Broken fragments of names, but they have meanings. And they are very old names, yours.'

'As old as Ago?' asked Niko.

'Much older. Much. From the time of the first Olympics, thousands of years before Ago. But Greeks are tenacious. They hang on to things.'

'Hellas. Which the rest of the world calls Greece. Yes.'

'Tell us our names then,' said Peri.

'Peri. From Pericles; he was a great leader in Athens, time before time, before time . . .'

'What about me? What about Niko?' Niko cried, clapping his hands.

'Nike for victory, I imagine. And Cal here is called for Calliope, who was a kind of spirit, and moved men to write books . . . or perhaps she is Caledon, the swallow, that comes with spring.'

'And Cassie?' we asked, calling her name all together, full of excitement. I had never known that names could mean things! And I was pleased to be a lovely thing like a bird of spring.

'She is Cassandra, I think,' he said, looking at her very gravely. 'Cassandra, in the old books, could see the future. She told it truly, but it did not save her. You should be wary of your gift, girl.'

'I try not to use it,' she said.

'But you have it?'

142

'Only a little, I think. It isn't like seeing, more like feeling frightened . . . feeling that something is there that I haven't seen . . . Could you take it away for me?'

'No. I don't think so.'

'What does Philip's name mean?' piped up the urchin.

'That's interesting,' the scholar said. 'I think he must be called for Philippides, and I know a story about him . . .'

'Oh, tell us the story!' cried Niko.

'Tell us, and when we rescue him we can tell him, and he won't mind so much having missed seeing you,' I said.

'He won't mind anyway,' said Peri. 'He doesn't mind anything much except winning.'

'Well, I miss him,' said Cassie, making me look sharply at her in surprise. 'I'd like to know his story to tell him.'

'Fill your beakers, then, and settle down, and I'll tell you,' the scholar said.

And this is what he told us.

'In the far long past, hundreds of years before Ago, there was a war in your country. The Hellenes had offended a great king, and he brought thousand upon thousand of fighting men to crush them, and to take their land for himself. He came to attack the men of the city of Athens above all, because they had defied him – they had even put his messengers to death.'

'Why did they do that?' piped up the urchin.

'Because the messengers brought a demand for surrender,' the scholar said. 'Now before the great King arrived the Athenians made treaties with other cities in Greece, and especially with the Spartans, who were great fighters – not as good as the Athenians at any of the arts of peace and government, but marvellous and famous soldiers – and the Spartans agreed that they would march out and fight the great King alongside the Athenians when the attack came. And so when the news reached Athens that the sea was covered in ships to the horizon, and that soldiers of the great

King were landing in their shiploads and camping on the plains of Marathon, the Athenians chose a fine runner – the fastest man in the city – to run the miles to Sparta, and bring the help that the Spartans had promised to give. And the man they chose was called Philippides.

'So Philippides set out to run to Sparta. It was a hundred and fifty miles, mountainous nearly all the way, and it took him two days. But when he got to Sparta they were keeping a festival; worshipping a god, something to do with the moon. They told him they would not come at once, but at the end of the moon's phase, when their sacred days and nights were over. So then Philippides realized that his people would have to face the vast army of invaders all alone, because of course the generals of the great King would soon learn that no help was coming for four days; they would be certain to attack before help could reach the Athenians. And so he turned round and ran back, to warn the men of his city. He ran back through the dry hills, and he saw visions as he went. A god appeared to him, with messages; Philippides ran on. He got back in two and a half days with his awful news, but he had pushed himself past the limits, and when he reached Athens he dropped dead in the market-place, having spoken his warning.'

'He just died?' said Niko, softly.

'But his name lived on. The Athenians built a shrine in the heart of their city to the god Pan who had spoken to him on his run; and because of him, when the Olympic Games were begun again in the Ago, the longest race was called the Marathon. And it must be his name that was given to your friend in the village he comes from . . . surely.'

'Is that all?' I asked.

'That's all about Philippides,' the scholar said.

'Then tell us another story; tell us what happened in the battle!' said Cassie.

'The Athenians won the battle anyway, without the

Spartans,' said the scholar gleefully. 'They had a clever general, and a clever battle plan, and the weight of numbers was no use against their discipline and brains. But here's a good bit – you'll like this, I know – about goats!'

'Goats?' we chorused, amazed.

'Goats aren't any good at fighting, scholar!' I piped up.

He laughed. 'Listen, listen,' he said. 'The night before the battle the Athenian generals were camped in the hills, across the road to Athens, looking down at the plain of Marathon, and it was bright with the campfires of their enemies, like the night sky in summer with stars. So they promised their goddess that they would sacrifice to her one goat for every dead enemy found lying on the plain the next evening; and then they couldn't keep the promise – can you guess why?'

'Tell us! tell us!' we called to him. All round the circle of light cast by fire and the torch our faces were bright and eagerly bent on him.

'They hadn't got enough goats!' he cried. 'There weren't enough goats in all their lands and hills. They had to pay them off at several dozens a year, and they were still paying when they were conquered and engulfed, nearly two centuries later.'

'But they had beaten their enemy for good,' said Peri.

'Oh no, not at all,' the scholar said. 'He came back for more. They defeated him twice, and then fell to fighting each other, and of course, the Spartans won . . .'

'So after all it's a sad story, in the end,' said Cassie.

'Perhaps,' said the scholar. 'More a kind of warning, I think. A warning that wasn't taken.'

'What is sadder than that . . .' she murmured to herself.

'And time to sleep now; I'm too old to spin the night away sitting by the fire like this,' the scholar said.

'Will you tell me, before we sleep, what my name means?' said Dio.

'I wondered about that. I thought of an Emperor called Diocletian; but I think you are Diogenes, young man. And he was a mad thinker who carried a lantern in daylight; who carried a lamp through the world, looking, he said, for an honest man. That must be you, don't you think?'

'But it can't be,' said Dio. 'I was named Dio as a babe in arms; I have carried the name from long before the torch was given me, when my parents had no way of knowing what would happen that day . . . It can't be.'

'Well then, it is just blind chance, and means nothing,' the scholar said, 'if you would rather think so.'

'I'm afraid of this either way,' said Dio.

'Of course you are,' the scholar said. 'But I must give you goodnight.'

In the darkness of the hall at night, while we were sleeping on the straw, and the fire was a scatter of dim embers, and the torch had quietened to a little blue flame, I whispered to Dio.

'Dio, we aren't really looking for an honest man, are we? I thought it was honest Games we were looking for.'

'We were looking for somewhere where the torch belonged. I suppose I thought there might be, somewhere, a little left of Ago; people who understood it . . .'

'The scholar said he couldn't tell us anything about the torch.'

'Perhaps we should ask him instead about Ago. Tomorrow we will. And then I think we must return to the road Brameen knows, and keep on.'

'Dio? Do you think there is a way to rescue Philip?'

'Brameen says he knows one. But he will not tell me about it yet. Just as Cassie won't tell me things . . .'

I lay awake for a while thinking about that. 'I will ask her; I haven't forgotten,' I said, softly, so as not to wake the others. But Dio seemed to be already asleep.

Fifteen

In the morning, though I thought we woke early, the scholar was already at his books. We tumbled into his lake to wash, and breakfasted on yesterday's bread and the new morning's milk, which Sancho had already fetched down the hillside from the scholar's goats, and ladled out to us from a wooden pail. It was warm and rich, and coated our lips as we drank.

'We can't stay here long,' Dio said. 'It isn't fair. He doesn't have much, and we'll eat him out of house and home.'

'But we can talk to him more before we go?'

'We can stay just one more day, I think. If we work for our supper.'

And Sancho let us work. There was a little trickling spring that needed cleaning out to run faster; there was wood to chop, and a garden of lettuces and carrots to be weeded. We earned another night's lodging; and a chance, when he emerged into the late afternoon light and sat in the mellow sunshine, blinking, to sit down at the scholar's feet under his fig tree, and talk to him some more.

And this time Dio asked him what we had often wondered – what happened to Ago? Where did all the wonder-working go to? What disaster had carried it all away?

'Was it an earthquake?' Niko piped up. 'Was it a flood?'

'Neither of those,' the scholar said. 'I'm working on this. I've been trying to find the answer to this for many, many years. That's what led me to books in the first place . . .'

'Is it something very hard to find?' I asked.

'The trouble is that they didn't understand it themselves,' the scholar said. 'When it was happening they didn't know how to stop it; they didn't know how much would be lost . . . I can read their cries of woe, their accusations and resolutions, I can learn how hard they tried to keep what they had got, to go on using the knowing . . . but I can't see exactly whey they failed.'

'Haven't you found out anything about it?' said Dio, sadly.

'Very little,' the scholar said.

'Tell us the little,' said Peri.

'In the Ago there were two divisions of the world,' the scholar said. 'A little like the Athenians and the Spartans, really. The Spartans were great soldiers, but most of the marvels were made by the Athenians. The Athenians – that's just my name for them, you understand – were men of many nations, but they all spoke English. That's why we do, to this day. The marvels included the weapons they made to fight each other . . . they speak of these weapons as though they would bring the end of the world. They were very afraid of them.'

'I didn't know the Ago people might have been afraid,' I said. 'When you think of what they could do . . .'

'People are always afraid because of what they can't do,' the scholar said. 'They weren't wizards and witches, back in the Ago. They were subject to bad luck, and illness, and death, just like us. They became afraid of the weapons to the point where the Athenians abandoned them. Disarmed themselves.'

'What happened then?' asked Dio.

'What you would expect. The Spartans took over the world. Then the time of marvels was over, and the wonders began to crumble away.'

'But why? Why should that have happened?'

'The Spartans themselves didn't know why it happened. They kept trying to stop it. I can read the orders their chieftains gave, volume after volume of them, all trying to keep things going . . .'

'Then, why?' Dio asked him.

'I think it has something to do with what I told you yesterday. The wonders needed many people working together. The Spartans made people work together by giving them orders, as if they were soldiers in an army. But the orders weren't right – they were too simple. They came from people who didn't know enough. I think in the Ago you couldn't run things by giving orders; you had to let people choose to do things.'

'How could they work together if they were all choosing for themselves?' asked Peri.

'In your village,' the scholar said, 'far away in the land of the ancients, how do people decide when to plough, when to harvest, what to plant in fields and gardens? Does someone give orders?'

'Of course not!' Peri said. 'Each one can see what needs doing in their own field . . .'

'And what if the well needs repair – the one that everyone uses? Who gives orders?'

'Everyone agrees. There is a meeting; sometimes a lot of argument. Then it gets done with everyone helping.'

'An Athenian way,' the scholar said. 'If someone gave orders, if nothing was ever done except because an order had been given which it would be death to disobey, then perhaps the well would get mended more quickly . . .'

'Or perhaps the well would not get mended at all,' said Cassie suddenly. 'I think I understand that.'

'Well, I don't!' said Peri. 'What contemptible fools and cowards the Ago Athenians were, that they would rather let the world fall into this misery and poverty, sooner than fight

149

their enemies, and stand up for themselves like men! Look at us now; struggling along, knowing nothing, having almost nothing, and troubled all the time, disturbed by knowing what people once had, what they could once do! Disarmed themselves, did they? And let the people of the future turn into the poor relations of the past!'

'I thought like that, at first,' the scholar said. 'Sometimes when I am reading and I read of wonders, I think like that. But then I come outside and sit in the evening sun, and eat a fig from my tree, and I think to myself: What do I know? How do I know that they were wrong to be afraid? Perhaps I would not be here, eating figs, sunning my ignorance, listening to the birdsong in the dusk, if what they feared had come about.'

'But, scholar,' said Peri, protesting, 'nothing – *nothing* that happened all that time ago could have stopped figs growing, or the sun shining now!'

We all watched him reach up for a fig, and pull it open, and eat it, as though we were watching a wonder. 'But nothing could make pictures fly through the air, or mechanical birds carrying people, or take men to the moon and back again,' the scholar said, 'and we believe all that. This I am sure of,' he went on. 'What has happened once can happen twice. What was once known can be known again. If we want the wonders of Ago, and if we strive for them, we can achieve them again.'

'Surely we can't,' said Dio. 'How could we achieve what we can barely imagine?'

'One step at a time, perhaps. After all, the torch has come again, and till yesterday I wouldn't have imagined that.'

'But that wasn't from knowing anything, from any wonderful thing happening, or striving, or any of that!' said Dio. 'It was only because of us!'

'Well, yes,' said the scholar, 'that's what I'm saying.'

Dio wandered off by himself, after that. We were all ready to eat, with a fine fire burning, and everyone cheerful, and he had not returned. So I went to look for him.

He was sitting on the beach of the scholar's lake, his chin cradled in his hands. I sat down beside him, and said nothing at first. Then I said, 'Supper's ready.'

He said, 'The scholar and Brameen have been talking over things. They've got a route planned out for getting to the Province faster – going by boat some of the way.'

'That's good,' I said.

'Maybe. But what if the Province puts out the torch for good?'

'I must admit, sort of guessing on past form, I don't think the torch will like races with slaves,' I said.

'I have been trying to tell myself that we needn't bother with Philip. But I think we must. Even if we do lose the torch; I keep telling myself that we once got on fine without even knowing there was such a thing . . .'

'That was when we were children. But ever since you began to carry the torch . . .'

'I am a prisoner to it. Yes, I know. And Philip is a real pain; not my favourite person. But if he hadn't come with us he wouldn't be in trouble, Cal, and after all, the torch is only a thing, for all the fuss people make of it, and Philip is . . .'

'Someone!' I said, and threw my arms round him. 'Of course,' I cried, 'of course!', pulling him to his feet, and dancing round him like a madcap. 'Come and have supper, and in the morning let's get ourselves to the Province as fast as we can!'

Sixteen

As quickly as we could was not quick. It took us three months, from the scholar's tower to the race-courses of the Province. Three months of marching, sometimes begging, sometimes buying our lodging; then a crossing from a little coastal port in a fishing-boat that could barely cram us all on board, and needed to wait for a flat calm to risk it; then another shore, another pitch in the voices around us, once more strange-sounding names. This newest land we had entered, however, was rich, with good farmland, growing wheat and vines, and the people having ponies and carts, and looking prosperous. The races, we were told, were at Ex and that is where we went.

The nearer we got to Ex, the more confident Brameen became. He began to recognize roads, and a hillside, on which he said he had trained when he was a runner. 'I know the way now,' he told us, round a campfire a little off the road, where we were cooking a meal and intending to sleep for the night. 'Two more days at most.'

'When are you going to tell us the plan for saving Philip?' Niko asked.

'When you have seen for yourself how difficult it will be,' said Brameen.

And when we got there, we did see. The roads into Ex were jammed with people, all in holiday dress and mood, all thronging to see the races, and eagerly talking together about possible winners, certain losers. We mixed with them, hoping our road-worn garments wouldn't draw attention to us, among so many in their best and brightest clothes. Once a group of travellers accosted us, demanding to know why we carried a torch – for the torch was burning steadily in Dio's hands – and Peri replied that it was to light the campfire we needed to settle down by at night. We were listening eagerly for any sound of Philip's name, but we didn't hear it. Everyone was betting that a runner called Tornado would carry off the honours. Once we were in the town, Brameen took us through back streets to a shabby inn with a courtyard and scruffy rooms opening on it, and was greeted at once by the innkeeper as an old friend. 'Never thought to see him again,' he kept telling us, shaking his head. 'I owe your friend Brameen a good deal, a good deal . . .' Even so, the inn was full of out-of-town racegoers; he could find us only three little rooms, and the grassy orchard for our followers to camp in.

Brameen found a sharp-eyed, skinny boy who had joined us just before we visited the scholar, and told him to make, little by little, a hole in the thorn hedge at the back of the orchard, and keep it covered over with bundles of the cut branches. 'That gives on to the open country,' he said. 'We might need that.'

'Everyone knows so much about these races,' Peri complained, 'we must stick out like sore thumbs . . .'

'Use it, use it,' Brameen said. 'Keep telling people it's your first time and ask them questions . . . find out all you can.'

'What did you do for the innkeeper that makes him so fond of you?' Cassie asked. For already we could see that he had turned away customers prepared to pay heavily for the rooms he had given us. The inn was thronged with people, the courtyard full of ponies, and more folk were arriving every minute.

'Nothing,' Brameen said.

'Oh, stop kidding and tell us, Brameen!' said Niko.

'Nothing,' said Brameen. 'But he laid a small bet on me against very long odds once, and I won the race. He bought this inn with the money.'

And we soon saw what sort of a hero Brameen had been. When the inn filled up with a throng of people eating and drinking at nightfall, the innkeeper began to brag. 'It's all very well for you youngsters with short memories,' he said, shaking his head as he drew wine from his barrels. 'You carry on about Tornado and Zipper, and all these newfangled slave runners – "speeds", as you call them. I bet you've never even heard of Brameen.'

'Beat the record in the Ex Prize fifteen years ago,' said someone from the corner seat.

'My dad was saying he would've beaten the Tornado,' a young man said. 'If you'd believe it!'

'Well, friend,' said the innkeeper, relishing the moment and turning to Brameen, 'could you have beaten the Tornado?'

A huge excited uproar broke out. The customers shouted and yelled at each other and at Brameen, began to remember wins and losses in bets they had laid when he was running, and began to fight each other to buy him drinks. 'I can't say, I can't say,' Brameen was saying when we could hear him again above the din. 'I haven't seen the Tornado. I'll tell you tomorrow. What's the competition, then? Isn't there a Greek runner – something beginning with fff . . . can't remember exactly.' But nobody seemed to recognize that. There wasn't anyone with short odds against the Tornado, we gathered; but there were runners called Zipper and Radio Rays with an outside chance.

The talk went on late, and it was late before Brameen, with wine on his breath, came to bed.

Even so, he woke us very early. He wanted just a few of

us to come with him. Dio, and Peri, and Niko. 'And Cal can come too,' he said. 'We're going to suss out the ground. You must leave that torch behind.'

'Where will it be safe, if we have to leave it?' I asked.

'We'll hide it in the orchard,' Brameen said.

So we went out into the dew and sharp chill of the morning, under the apricot trees, to the corner by the thorn hedge where our companions were asleep. We built a new fire by setting the torch upright and propping boughs all round it, so that it looked like the flame on the top of a bonfire.

'No one will notice it at first glance,' Brameen said.

'But one of us must stay with it,' said Dio. 'I cannot leave it in the keeping of newcomers . . .'

'Let Cassie stay,' said Brameen. 'She looks least like a runner among you. And the rest of you are my trainees for the morning.'

Brameen took us to a fenced and guarded ranch. It was a little way outside the town. At first the gatekeeper wouldn't let us in, and we were left staring at the high walls topped with bundles of thorn, and the stout gates braced with iron strapping; but Brameen demanded that his name be sent in to the owner. Soon a man came out to us, dressed in elaborate satin clothes. Shaking Brameen by the hand, and calling him 'my old villain', he led us through the gate. Brameen was calling the man 'Bruno', and joking with him . . . soon he said that he was earning a living, now, by training slaves for re-sale as speeds. He hoped that Bruno would let his young hopefuls see the morning exercise, to get some idea of what a real runner looked like at close quarters. Of course he couldn't buy tickets for us in the pavilion; it would cost too much.

Bruno looked us over. He stared at Peri, stooped and pinched his calves, grabbed his chin, and pulled his mouth open and looked in. 'This one's strong enough,' he said. Dio bridled and flinched when Bruno turned to him. 'Too nervy,' said Bruno, turning away. Then it was my turn. 'Promising', I was called. 'But is there anywhere where they run girls?'

'I heard it was the up-and-coming thing in the north,' said Brameen.

'Quite disgusting,' said Bruno. 'But now, what you've really come to see is Tornado on his morning warm-up – right?'

He led us into a yard; a spacious yard, with a level track surfaced with beaten sand. On to this yard there gave a row of sheds with bolted doors. A man sauntered up to us wearing brown cloth, and carrying a little wand with a steel spike on it. 'This is my trainer,' Bruno said. 'Who was it in your day?'

'We called him Caligula,' said Brameen, and Bruno laughed.

We were trailing along behind the three men, moving past the rows of stable doors.

'We'll have Tornado first,' said Bruno.

And opening the upper half of a door, he showed us, within, a stall. It was immaculately clean. Fresh straw on the floor, a window high in the back wall, a tap with a chained cup hanging beside it . . . Standing inside was a naked youth. Philip.

The trainer's spur flicked round Philip's ankles. 'Easy does it,' Bruno said. 'I don't want a scratch on him.'

'No need, with this one,' the trainer said. 'Got the taste for it, he has . . .' and indeed Philip flew round the track, his thrumming footfalls like a wild drummer, his whole body moving with a rhythm of speed. I don't know how many laps he ran, but at last they let him stop, and he leant his hands on his knees, panting from exertion, even his breathing smooth. He stared at us blankly. Only for a tiny second did his eyes meet mine.

Bruno and Brameen were sitting under a canvas shade, drinking wine, watching speeds brought naked from their stalls. We had been given water, and were sitting at the edge of the track. Brameen came over to us, and began to point and talk about the runners. Softly, in the middle of the loud talk, he slipped something into my hand, and murmured, 'Go and give him this, and tell him to choose.' I glanced down at what he had given me. A little stubby knife, with a silver handle and a blue-black blade.

'I paid a king's ransom for him, and he's won it back for me five times over,' Bruno was saying. 'Wins every time, that one. Only, my friend, you won for me too in your time; so I'm just giving you the nudge – very quietly – right? Don't bet on him today.'

I was walking out of earshot. I wandered around the track, as though just bored with sitting. Philip was leaning over the lower half of his stall door, his eyes blank. He watched me coming, pretending not to see. Then I leant over his door, and dropped the knife into the straw. 'Brameen says you have to choose,' I said. 'But he didn't say what . . .'

Suddenly the trainer was beside me. 'You haven't been feeding him, have you?' he demanded. 'Mustn't feed them before a race. Clear off now, and let him rest.'

I removed myself smartly. And soon Brameen took his leave, beckoned us, thanked Bruno profusely, and led us out on to the street. We bought bread and olives and a disc of soft white cheese from street vendors as we went, and took the food up to the orchard to share it with those we had left waiting.

We sat round the dummy fire, talking. 'What was all that about, Brameen?' Dio demanded. 'Why did that man let us in like that, and show us Philip?'

'It's a godsend to him,' Brameen said. 'Real disinterested witnesses who will say that the runner was in good health and running superbly just before the race . . . he could have kissed me for bringing you . . .'

'But why shouldn't Philip be well?'

'Didn't you hear him warning me not to bet? Your friend is going to lose this afternoon. Bruno will have bet heavily against him.'

'You mean it's fixed?' Cassie said.

'With all that money at stake? Of course it's fixed.'

'It'll be easier said than done to get Philip to lose,' said Dio.

I was staring absentmindedly at the torch. It flickered below the piled-up logs we had laid round it, and a thin thread of smoke rose into the overarching boughs of the tree.

'So much the worse for him,' said Brameen.

'And I don't understand why you made me give him a knife!' I cried. 'What can he do with one small knife? He couldn't cut a halter with that, never mind break out of that stall! It wouldn't cut anything . . .'

'He will know what it will cut, if he wants to get out of there,' said Brameen grimly.

And the fine thread of smoke from the torch faded into the shadows of the tree.

Dio grabbed it, pulled it out of the pile of branches; Cassie let out a wail of dismay. As Dio seized the torch the mecho that had so baffled us fell into the cone, out of sight. We could see a blackened, empty hollow in the core of the torch, where all this time the mysterious fuel had been. Dio handed it to Peri, and Peri handed it to me. And we could all see that this time it meant disaster; the torch was not only out, but cold; not only cold, but broken.

And, 'If it was truth-telling that put it out,' said Brameen sternly, 'You are better without it.'

'Torch or no torch,' Dio said, 'We must go and get Philip.'

'We must be there in case he chooses to come,' said Brameen. 'But he might not choose. You must be ready for that; it is a lot to ask.'

'Won't you tell us, now, what you mean?' I said. 'And what you thought would come of giving him a little knife?'

'You saw for yourselves how it is. He is well guarded. To free him would be hard and very dangerous, and besides, he is worth a fortune to his owner; there would be a hue and cry after us to the ends of the Province, and into the northlands, and we would be thieves on the run. We would be caught. The only way to freedom is to become useless as a runner, as I did when I fell and lamed myself. When it is very clear you cannot run again, they throw you out.'

'So, with that knife . . .' said Cassie, slowly.

'But he would never run again . . .' I remembered the blank face and shuttered eyes of Philip in his stall.

'He won't do anything that stops him running,' said Niko.

'But this afternoon his owner wants him to do badly,' said Brameen.

'Brameen, how will they make him lose?' Dio asked.

'They'll threaten terrible punishment. He might prefer that knife. But whatever he does, we must be there. Come now.'

Moosyer Bruno had found seats for us in his pavilion. We sat high up at the back, where we could see the great sweep of the race-course, the thronging people, the stalls for placing bets, each with a little banner on a pole to make itself seen above the press of people, and beyond, the blue hills that circled Ex. Philip's race was the last one in the programme, and carried the most majestic prize. So we sat and watched runners win and lose below us; we were sitting near the line that served for both start and finish. After each race a crowd of happy gamblers seized a man and carried him shoulder high along the stands, waving and hallooing. It was not the nearly naked runner that they carried and cheered, it was the owner.

When the last race was called, some dozen runners were led out. Philip looked up at the crowd, and I thought he saw us. I waved; I hoped he saw us. His trainer was standing just behind him, leaning over his shoulder, talking to him. The runners fidgeted, and then stooped, lodged their feet on starting blocks, braced themselves . . . a gun was fired.

And Philip flew away from the starting line, going like the wind. There has surely never been anyone who ran like him; he ran as birds fly and fishes swim, he ran with such harmonious movement that you saw, every time you watched him, what limbs and trunk are for, you saw why a body is built and jointed and hinged and balanced that way. While he was running you saw how beautiful humankind is, you felt your own limbs apt for speed, your own frame finely made like the wonders of Ago. Philip flew round the track. Below us I could see the flush of anger staining the thick neck of his owner, the hands clenched furiously on the rail . . . but that man did not own Philip; each lovely thrumming stride he took proved it. He did not make the smallest attempt to lose, he did not trouble even to make it close; he left the others far behind, and came in easily the victor . . .

The crowd went wild with joy. Obviously they had laid their bets on Tornado to win. They heaved Bruno up, and began to carry him along in the press of people. The runners, their chests heaving, were left standing as the triumphant people carried Bruno away. A space opened round Philip. He was holding something aloft; something bright – the knife! It glinted in his hand. Then he stooped, and, graceful to the last, drew it in a great sweep across the back of his own knees, and fell at once, crumpled, on to the sand.

Seventeen

At nightfall we went looking for him. We had got back to our orchard in the confusion, keeping out of Bruno's way. Then we split into twos and threes, and began to search the back alleys and rubbish dumps. Near Bruno's house was the least likely place, according to Brameen. The town was buzzing with excitement, gleeful gossip spilling loudly out of every alehouse. Of course it had got out that Bruno had bet against Philip; of course Philip was a hero to every poor man who had laid a sou that he would win. Everyone in the town, it seemed, would have known that it would be no good asking a slave of that mettle to lose on purpose . . . everyone in the town assumed the slave would by now be dead.

But he wasn't dead. Nearly; but not quite. We found him in the end lying on the rubbish from a road-sweeper's cart, beaten black and blue, and unconscious. We carried him back to our orchard, and washed and covered his wounds as best we could, with a pan of water from the inn and a torn-up shirt of Brameen's. Brameen held him tenderly, touched him tenderly, helped Cassie dab and bandage him. 'What defiance!' he murmured. 'I would never have thought of that! To win first!'

'Will he get better?' asked Niko, near to tears.

'Better? He'll live,' said Brameen. 'And he'll walk again, one day. But he cut his own hamstrings; he'll never run again . . . I'll have to show him basket-work before I leave you.'

'When are you leaving us?' asked Dio.

'I have kept my bargain with you already, since I have

brought you here and shown you what way there was to free
your friend,' said Brameen. 'But I will stay with you till we
have crossed out of the Province again; this isn't any place
for those who don't know its ways. We'll rest for three days
while Philip recovers a bit; and we'll lie low; then we'll go as
fast as we can to whatever border you choose. And I'll see
you safely across it.'

So we had three evenings to talk it over, sitting at the top
end of the orchard, round a fire, roasting our supper over
the flames and thinking about it.

We all thought the torch would not re-light while we were
still in the Province. It was the urchin who set us on our next
goal. 'It's an Ago thing, innit?' he said, jerking a thumb at
the torch. 'It wants to be where Ago was, maybe?'

'What do you mean?' Dio asked him. 'Ago was a time, not
a place, wasn't it? Wasn't it everywhere?'

'Not so's you'd notice, it weren't,' the urchin said. 'Them
places what we've been in since you rescued me in Corfoo.
Ago never happened much in any of them. People in the
desert, and all them places, what they're doing is mostly
what they was always doing, before Ago. You want to see
what it looks like where the Ago people really had it going
for them – like what it looks like on the Island.'

'But how do you know all this, urchin?' I asked him. 'How
do you know what it looks like?'

'Born there,' said the urchin.

'But how did you get to Corfoo, if you were born on some
other island, far in the north?' Cassie asked him.

'I was took as a slave,' he said. 'I could juggle pebbles,
and sing a song. But when they got me to Corfoo no one
wanted me; saw it once and had enough, they had. So them
that'd got me couldn't sell me, so they gave me the push, and
I went for a beggar.'

'You poor thing,' said Cassie softly.

'And this place you were stolen from . . .' said Dio.

'I weren't stolen!' said the urchin indignantly. 'I got more sense than to get stolen! Me mam sold me.'

'Tell us about the Island,' said Dio, gently.

'Horrible place really,' the urchin said. 'But it's full of bashed-up and broken bits of Ago. Socking great buildings, half fallen down, and metal towers, all rusty, and mower-ways and all.'

'And pictures in the air, and flying chariots . . .' said Niko, wistfully.

'Nah,' said the urchin. 'Only bust-up places.'

'Are there races anywhere on the Island?' asked Peri.

'There's races of horses, I think,' the urchin said. 'There might be races for men, for all I know.'

'We'd better go there,' said Dio. 'How far is it?'

Of course we would never have set out for the Island if we'd known how far it was. If we'd known we would still be walking when winter came, and would walk through spring and summer . . . above all, we would not have aimed at the Island if we had known that the torch had deserted us; that its bright and cheering light would not shine on a single step of the way.

But we knew none of that, and so set out.

Brameen came with us to the northern edges of the Province and then turned back, going back to dusty Africa, and his daughter.

We expected Ahmet to go with Brameen, but though he parted from his countryman with tears, and was very quiet and unsmiling for miles and days after that, he came with us. He was useful; though he had learned so few words of English and spoke them lisping, he was patient and tender with Philip, and good at making friends for us. Sitting by the campfire at night he carved and twisted little dolls, whittled out of wood and with straw hair, and gave them to children along the way. The country changed; no more vines, no more olives grew. The nights got steadily colder, and though the sun shone on some of our days, it became, little by little, a cooler sun. And little by little we were fewer. In twos and threes many of those who had joined us when we were marching bravely towards the Province, with the torch burning, turned back for home. Sometimes they found work on the farms of the cool plains, bringing in the harvest or tending the beasts. Some said they were staying only for a day or two, only for a week's wages, and would catch us up later . . . but we did not expect them. In some ways it was easier to be few again, to need to find only a dozen suppers, to strike the people whose land we walked through as nothing but a handful of vagrants, unremarkable, who could pass on their way without trouble . . .

But of course there was trouble in our own hearts. Philip grieved all the time about the torch, could not bear to see the poor dead thing thrust into a saddle-bag on one of our donkeys, wanted to carry it himself if Dio wasn't carrying it. Philip rode many miles before he walked one; though in the end he could limp along somehow, leaning on a stick. By campfires in the endless hillsides we heard his story. He had thought of refusing the cruel release that the knife offered him; thought of accepting that he would always be Bruno's runner . . . 'It was very hard and bitter for me,' he said, 'to think that I would never run again . . . but then running to lose for Bruno, or even to win for such a man, was not what my speed was made for. I have been sick at heart to think of the twisted races, the crooked and terrible things we have seen on our journey; and I remembered that the rest of you serve the torch, though you have no hope of victory; none of you can win a race . . . and yet you have all bravely suffered and journeyed for the sake of a racer's sign . . . So I thought: I will serve the torch the way these others serve it, the way a loser serves it, better to be a cripple and go with the torch than a victor in a contemptible cause . . .'

When Philip talked in this way, Dio was thrown into the deepest misery because the torch was out. And of course he looked to Cassie to tell him at last what she thought was good for the torch . . . and Cassie still would not tell him.

'It will make it harder for you; it will make it worse if you know,' she said.

'How could it be worse?' he said. We were walking then in a flat and desolate plain, swept with cold rainstorms, and the darkness came earlier each evening, and the morning later. The people had gathered their crops into barns, and were huddled by their fires with nothing to spare for strangers. Sometimes they would give us shelter in the cow-byres and hay-stalls; sometimes not even that.

I was sorry for Dio; I was sorry for us all. I too began to bully Cassie, to implore her to tell me.

'You'll be sorry if I do,' she said.

In the end I said, 'All right, let me be sorry. Anything rather than being sorry about you – anything rather than having to think you don't care, you won't help us . . .'

She bit her lip, and there were tears in her eyes. We were walking facing into a bitter wind. 'You're forcing me,' she said. 'And no good ever comes of forcing people; you more than any of us should know that . . .'

'All right, then I'm forcing you,' I said, stubbornly.

'Supposing you were singing to yourself,' she said. 'Supposing you were singing to yourself, and I told you the torch liked that. What would you do?'

'I'd grab it and I'd sing to it like fury!' I said.

'Why would you?' she said.

'Well, to get it to light up, of course,' I said, bewildered.

'It wouldn't be the same sort of singing,' she said. 'It wouldn't work. Think about it.'

'But we supposed you had just told me it would work, Cassie . . .'

'No,' she said. 'Think some more. But if you get it, Cal,

whoever lights that thing up again, it won't be you, just as it won't, it hasn't been, me.'

I walked along, head bent, eyes smarting in the cold, breathing into the collar of my cloak, which was slowly covered with a rime of frozen breath.

'Do you mean that if you do something specially to light the torch, it won't work?' I asked her at last.

'If you did something specially for it, that would be a reason,' she said. 'It doesn't like reasons.'

'But why not just tell Dio that?'

'*Think* about it,' she said. I thought about it. While I was thinking we reached the shelter of a little leafless wood, offering a wind-break of a kind. A cold mist had gathered on the land, and it was getting dark. We halted our little cavalcade, tied the donkeys where they could graze on frozen grass, and began to gather kindling and put up our tent.

I was still thinking about it when we had eaten our scant supper and were lying in our damp blankets, waiting for sleep. Once you knew the torch didn't like reasons, then you would know that anything you tried because you wanted it to light again would fail. For something to work, it would have to be something that you were doing not to light the torch; not for anything. I longed for the torch right in my frozen marrow-bones; I remembered how it had warmed us when we were freezing in the open boat; how it had cheered us, and been a reason for what we did . . . *it* was a reason, even if it didn't like reasons . . . I yearned and yearned for it to shine again, to be with us again . . . but I did see that it wouldn't help to tell Dio what Cassie knew about it. I did see that.

We were so cold. We were soaked to the skin, and slowly had taken on the colour of the sodden fields we trod across, their mud clinging to our clothes, getting on to our bedding, into our hair, under our fingernails. We had, of course, been cold before; but this was not the sharp, dry cold of the mountains, with their bright air, with the cleansing scour of the snow; it was clammy and dirty cold, fanned by a cruel wind. There were hills and valleys on this endless rolling plain, streams and rivers, but we could not bear the thought of washing ourselves in such bitter water, and so we marched on under a foul coating of mud, and when we were driven away from the edges of the villages by angry mobs – mostly of little boys – throwing stones, I could not blame them. No settled folk could be expected to like the look of us.

Though we lit fires at night with what wood we could find and huddled round them till the rain put them out, I took to getting up and running, going in wide circles round the camp, to warm up a bit before lying down shivering to sleep. And Philip began to teach me, telling me how to move arms and legs, how to lift my weight on the balls of my feet at each stride . . . I would never have let him teach me when he could run himself; now it was all the kindness I could give him to try out his instructions . . . poor boy. Ahmet was lame with a little grace – his lolloping steps, familiar to him from birth, did not break your heart to see, as seeing Philip's stiff and painful effort, as seeing the ugly lurching gait, knees crooked and face screwed up with pain, which was now all our splendid Nikathlon could manage.

A day came suddenly of softer weather. A thin sunlight shone, and we saw the nubbly little buds on the trees, a bright yellowing on willow boughs, and green blades standing above the thinning margins of snowdrifts. The birds sang frantically all day.

'There is such a thing as spring, then, in the far north,' said Peri. But the next day we came suddenly to the end of the land. We found ourselves on cliff-tops, with the sea

167

beneath us. Very faint and distant on the horizon, a blue shadow showed us another country, far offshore.

'You didn't tell us about this, urchin,' said Dio, appalled.

'Well, I told you it was called the Island, didn't I?' said the urchin, indignant.

'What do we do now?' I asked.

'Find a boat,' said the urchin, as though to an idiot.

It took the last of Philip's prize-money, and all we could get by selling our donkeys. The fishing-boat skippers who took us grumbled at the small amount we could pay, but took us just the same, making us sit on the fishes that filled the holds; little silver things as long as our fingers, lying thick and deep. We went in two boats that sailed for an hour out of sight of each other, and we were very glad to find ourselves still safe and still together on the stony beach where they landed us. A white cliff towered above the beach, just like the one on the other shore, and a gull with motionless wings glided on the brink of it.

We counted ourselves; what an odd lot we were! Fifteen filthy people, caked in mud and smelling of fish, and penniless . . . anyone could see that we would not be welcome visitors. You would need to know who we were to see any good in us. Dio, over there, haggard and worried, and barely able to look at the torch now, though he was this very minute checking that it was safe in his bundle. Peri, who was still strong and quiet; he had come all this way, though he didn't care a fig for the torch, I thought, because Dio was his friend. He might look like a ravenous bandit, but that was why he was here. Philip, looking like the theatrical beggars we had seen in the slave-market, with painted sores, and legs bent under them, the model broken limb extended instead – only the marks on his blotched skin were from real wounds, his crooked legs were his real ones. He had paid a high price to be here, struggling not to fall on the sliding shingle, instead of fettered comfortably. Niko, holding out a hand to help him; Niko who admired him still more for his famous runs than for his self-inflicted freedom. Ahmet, who was more than half dead with the cold, his golden skin blotched, his dark lips purple with it; he could have turned back anywhere on the way . . . he did not have to share his wealth with us until it all ran out. Cassie, silently staring at the grey, whale-backed water, rising and breaking. Cassie was always silent now. We had leaned on her too heavily, we had driven her into a corner by herself. She was younger than Niko, if I rightly remembered. Now she had the bird bones and swift excitable movements of a child, and the eyes of an old woman, staring. And then these others, some from the scholar's country, some from Ex, others whose names I had not learnt, but who must all have been crazy or wretched to cling to us, to come with us. And we all had mothers somewhere, who would have wept to see our state!

I said to Dio, 'We must stop, soon. We cannot go much further.'

And he said, 'We must let the urchin show us what he meant about Ago places.'

So we went on. We walked along the foot of the cliff till we came to a massive wall, built out into the ocean, with a squat little tower on the end. From there we could walk inland, following a valley. There were hundreds and hundreds of fallen-down houses, and a few kept mended and roofed by the fishermen; and once we were past the fishermen's quarter, we saw in that place only little children, keeping sheep pastured on the overgrown gardens.

Eighteen

There were Ago places on the Island. The most wonderful were what the urchin called 'mower-ways', great drove-roads along which the farmers led flocks of geese, flocks of sheep, herds of cattle to market in the towns. They looked as if some giant had taken two fingers and drawn a line on the land, like dragging your fingers in sand. The line made notches in hills, and ran along tall banks in valleys, and was smooth and easy walking all the way. Grassed over all the way. We wondered why they were so wide; the urchin thought it was to give grazing enough for the herds of beasts.

Hundreds of bridges crossed the mower-ways, some broken, but most usable. They were made solid; of stuff all in one piece, as though shaped in some kind of grey clay, like the mud houses of the desert edge. Where they had crumbled, rusting rods of iron emerged from the breaks, bent and tangled. Ahmet, in limping words learnt along the way, told us that the potters of his country used copper wires to strengthen pottery; this must be similar. The mower-ways went past places, rather than to them; you left them to go into towns. We didn't see any towns that weren't three-quarters empty, though there were markets in most of them where people sold eggs and vegetables, and homespun cloth, and there seemed always to be a blacksmith in a dark, smoky shed, making and mending tools. Although we found towns that were three or four days' walking time to cross, the people were living in them much as our people lived in

Hellas, though they were camped in patched and mended and propped remains of Ago houses, instead of having built their own. And nobody seemed to know or care about a torch; especially one that was out.

We moved very slowly and painfully. We had to forage for food, and we would go only as fast as Philip, which was very slow indeed until we found him a pony. The pony was a mangy and stunted creature, very squat and about the size of a donkey, which was offered us, to our amazement, in exchange for a desert saddle-bag we were carrying, made of red carpet. Our speed was improved to our own walking pace, and the relief of our feelings was very great; it had been terrible watching Philip struggle and sweat every step of the way.

We did find a horse-race at Newmark; it was mostly a horse-fair for buying and selling, but there were some races. We were told to keep clear of them; horses hated and feared fire, and if they caught a glimpse of a torch burning they would bolt. Had *we* caught a glimpse of our torch burning, we would have gone wild ourselves . . .

Beyond Newmark we had to turn back south-westerly, for the land was all under shallow water, growing sallows and rushes in a thousand lakes, and there were people living on islands and catching water-fowl, who walked home on long stilts to keep dry! We found a little high land, and a hilltop track, and began to follow it. All the time we were walking the weather was changing. Each morning it got light earlier; it got dark later. The days extended till they were longer by far than any days in Hellada. And the air became warmer. The sun shone fitfully from a sky always full of floating cloud, and we saw rainbows on the edge of showers. All around us trees were unfurling in brilliant green leaf, and flowers grew on the untended hillsides and along the banks of little tumbling streams. A time came when we were neither cold nor hungry, having washed and mended our tents, and fed well on rabbits for weeks past. The urchin made the first trap, but it was Ahmet who was best at setting them. We ate rabbits with potatoes stolen from the edge of fields. Once or twice we even earned food by working for a day or two on a farm; but we weren't welcome. When they wanted us to move on they came out with hay-forks and pick-handles, and stood staring while we bundled our things together, and scarpered.

But as we went west there were fewer people, fewer farms. You could see why; the land had become rocky and hilly, and less fertile-looking by far than the eastern plains. We were crossing sparsely inhabited hills covered with a scrubby purple plant, and with the sea appearing and disappearing on our right. In a deep cleft of these hills I found a waterfall one evening, a fierce and noisy little jet of water; I was standing under it, washing my hair, when Dio came by and saw me.

'I always liked your hair,' he said, watching as I twisted it, wringing the water out of it.

'You don't have to say that,' I said mechanically.

But instead of turning away, he answered me. 'I don't have to,' he said. 'I say what I like. Cal, if I hadn't been forced to choose you, it's you I would have chosen. Don't you know that? I can't help it that they forced me – forced us. It's what they always did.'

I sat down on a rock beside him, and thought about it. It could have been true. But I would never know. That's what's wrong with forcing people; you can't take it back and unforce them. What you have been forced to can't ever be freely chosen. Only there wasn't a lot of freedom around. What had we ever chosen freely? Did we choose to carry the torch to the ends of the earth? Perhaps we did; I could hardly remember, and now, I saw, it didn't matter *why* we did it, just that we *had* done it.

172

'You've been spending a lot of time running for Philip,' said Dio. 'Would you rather have him? Or Peri? Or Ahmet? I wouldn't stop you.'

'I might rather. I'll think about it. At least I would know it was my own doing.'

'Whereas back there, my father said if you didn't agree your father would beat you.'

'He didn't have to.'

'Mine neither. But they weren't worried what we thought; they only wanted the two olive groves run into one and farmed together.'

'I expect that's what they've done anyway, now we're gone,' I said, 'gone for ever.'

'Cal, I'll take you home again if it's what you want,' Dio said. 'Even if it takes half the rest of our lives.'

'We're taking the torch home,' I said. 'And it hasn't got there yet.'

'It's too late for the torch, I think,' he said. 'Everyone's forgotten about it. They're all too busy scraping a living. Even in these Ago ruins they don't know any more than we do, they haven't any more than we had. It's all lost and vanished.'

'There is the scholar.'

'Oh yes, there's him.'

'And the races the torch was meant for still might be just over the next hill . . .'

He smiled at me. 'Of course they might,' he said. 'But I'm supposed to be catching supper!' And he went on down beside the stream, whistling, with the bundle of spring-traps in his hand.

But on the other side of the lovely purple heights we came not to races, but once more to the end of the land. It was miles since we had seen any town or village, or even a lonely farm. And ahead of us we came down to a great golden strand, with huge and furious breakers beating on it. The beach was sheltered from the north by the jut of a tall headland, and tucked in beneath the headland was an abandoned place – a dozen stone houses, roofless now, but solidly built; a few fields stoutly walled, growing thistles and bracken, but cleared of stones. Above the houses a little wood clung to the foot of the hill, and a clear stream ran down through it and wound away across the sand. Beyond the wood the hillside ended in a tumble of rocks, and rock pools thick with mussels, there for the taking. A golden evening light showed us all this, and glowed richly on the retreating water, the subsiding waves, falling back and giving us more and more smoothed levels of sand. We stretched our tattered remnant of tent to make a roof on the smallest house, and Philip began to limp around, gathering kindling. Peri went down on the rocks picking mussels, and Cassie and I found an oven, built into the hearth of one of the houses. 'If we grew wheat we could make bread!' she said. We heard Niko's voice crooning and murmuring in the lean-to behind the house with the oven, and we found him there caressing a half-starved black bitch, her ribs sticking painfully proud under her skin, with a litter of puppies at her dugs.

'This one's Jason,' said Niko proudly, showing us, 'and that's Samson, and . . .'

'That's a bitch, Niko,' said Cassie, smiling. 'You can't call a bitch Samson. What's the mother called?'

'Mela,' he said. 'I'm going to find food for her.'

We left him to it, and wandered outside. The whole sky blazed for us, crimson and lemon and molten golden light, as the sun sank slowly down over endless ocean. Overawed by it, we gathered our meagre supper silently. We could all see that to the south there was more land; faint purple headlands jutting further than ours, a dusky shadow of even remoter land, even more distant journeys. But when Dio said, 'This is it. We can manage here. Surely we have done as much as the Guardian expected of us. We have done more than I expected of us,' nobody disagreed. The sun plunged into the distant water, only a thin rim of glory showing now.

Dio pulled the torch out of his bundle and set it upright, wedging it in the sandy soil of a little grassy bluff between village and beach, near the woodpile for the fire.

'The one thing I regret,' he said, 'is that it didn't come with us all the way.'

'If it had lasted long enough,' Cassie said, 'for us to light a fire from it here, we could have kept it burning for ever, couldn't we, and it would still have been the same fire . . .'

'Flame from the sun at Olim,' said Philip. 'Oh, if only . . .'

I stood with tears in my eyes, thinking of that. We could have kept the sun at Olim dancing brightly at every hearth, in every home for ever . . . my tears blurred the figures of Niko and the urchin dancing around at the edge of the waves, calling to each other, and laughing. They were lobbing pebbles into the curling crests of water . . . games still came easily to them . . .

Then they whooped and ran towards me. I had a dry stick in my hand, ready for the tinder-box, and I gave it to Philip. They ran, and called. 'Race you, Cal! Race you to the end of the beach!'

I swung on to tiptoe as Philip had taught me to do, I leant forward and ran, I ran for the sheer joy of the wide space, and the lovely light, and being called to join in . . . As I overhauled them the sun drowned, slid out of sight, and a deep purple light rolled over us, darkening. I ran. I heard the pounding footsteps of the boys behind me, and further behind sudden cries, sudden voices raised. What were they calling? The words reached me faintly in my flight – 'The torch!' So before I had measured even half the distance to the other headland I drew up, stopped, turned. The urchin was far behind; laughing gleefully, Niko shot past me, calling, 'I've won! I've won!' And I saw in the deepening darkness behind me a sudden blaze of glorious, fiery light, burning brilliantly, sending up shows of rainbow sparks, and almost as quickly expiring and vanishing from my sight, leaving me walking back under the lilac night, under the faint profusion of stars, towards the tiny spark of the new campfire, drawing me home with a promise of warmth and food.